Also by
GILES TIPPETTE . . .

WILSON'S GOLD . . . After years of running, one stake could put him back where he wanted. Or it could put him in the ground . . .

THE BANK ROBBER . . . When a man's land is stolen out from under him, he has to make a life any way he can . . .

CHEROKEE . . . Nothing can stop an honest man from settling a score . . .

DEAD MAN'S POKER . . . Outlaw life is a deadly game. But going straight is the biggest gamble of all.

GUNPOINT . . . There are two things more important than money: honor and survival . . .

SIXKILLER . . . No one fights harder than the man who fights for his kin.

HARD ROCK . . . Rough country breeds a rougher breed of man . . .

JAILBREAK . . . When a man's got his back against the wall, there's only one thing to do. Break it down.

AVAILABLE FROM JOVE BOOKS

Books by Giles Tippette

Fiction

THE BANK ROBBER
THE TROJAN COW
THE SURVIVALIST
THE SUNSHINE KILLERS
AUSTIN DAVIS
WILSON'S WOMAN
WILSON YOUNG ON THE RUN
THE TEXAS BANK ROBBING COMPANY
WILSON'S GOLD
WILSON'S REVENGE
WILSON'S CHOICE
WILSON'S LUCK
HARD LUCK MONEY
CHINA BLUE
BAD NEWS
CROSS FIRE
JAILBREAK
HARD ROCK
SIXKILLER
GUNPOINT
DEAD MAN'S POKER
CHEROKEE

Nonfiction

THE BRAVE MEN
SATURDAY'S CHILDREN
DONKEY BASEBALL AND OTHER SPORTING DELIGHTS
I'LL TRY ANYTHING ONCE

WILSON'S REVENGE

GILES TIPPETTE

JOVE BOOKS, NEW YORK

This Jove Book contains the complete
text of the original edition.
It has been completely reset in a typeface
designed for easy reading and was printed
from new film.

WILSON'S REVENGE

A Jove Book / published by arrangement with
the author

PRINTING HISTORY
Jove edition / June 1994

ISBN: 0-515-11214-3

A JOVE BOOK®
Jove Books are published by The Berkley Publishing Group,
200 Madison Avenue, New York, New York 10016.
JOVE and the "J" design are trademarks
belonging to Jove Publications, Inc.

PRINTED IN THE UNITED STATES OF AMERICA

10 9 8 7 6 5 4 3 2 1

To Doug Grad,
E.I.T.

WILSON'S REVENGE

ONE

⚮

Now I'll tell you, damn straight, that my plan, as our horses splashed their way across the Rio Grande, was to go into Mexico and rob every bank and fuck every woman and kill every sonofabitch that got in my way.

That was just about what my mood was.

We pulled up right as soon as we were across the river and dismounted and kind of stood around grinning at each other. Hell, it had been a damn hard run from the Panhandle, but we'd got away from there with better than $11,000 of that goddamn Skillet ranch's money and we'd made it the 500 miles to Mexico with no incident other than the piddling gunshot wound I'd taken under the collarbone.

Of course we wasn't *safe* in Mexico, but we was a hell of a lot safer than we'd been in Texas, especially up there in that north part of the country.

Well, we stood there looking at each other and I said, "Hell, let's take a rest and have a drink." I was talking to my two partners, Dennis Wilcey and the black Mexican, Chulo. We had just successfully robbed the payroll off an enormous ranch right outside of Tascosa and made a successful getaway back to the border country, which was my natural range.

I got a bottle of whiskey out of my saddlebags and uncorked, and then we passed it around, each man taking a pull, but holding the whiskey in his mouth until the others had theirs. Then we all swallowed at the same time and said, "Luck," as befits the toast.

Except for Chulo, who said, *"Buena suerte."* Him being a Mexican and not knowing no better.

Well, I'll tell you. I was feeling pretty good in spite of my mood, and my mood being hell-bent for leather. We had robbed the payroll and we'd made it to Mexico and we had money and we was still running free and loose.

And that ought to make any man feel pretty good. Fine, I was Wilson Young and I was wanted by about every law officer in two countries, but I was still walking around free and taking no man's orders. I was thirty-four years old and I'd been in the robbing and killing business for almost half of them years, but I hadn't chosen it. Indeed, I had done my dead level best on several occasions to get out of it.

But fate hadn't willed it that way.

So I was now goddamn well ready to say, "All right, I'm Wilson Young and I'm an outlaw. I didn't choose to be one, but since I am, I'm going to give it fits while I'm alive and at liberty."

We hunkered down on the ground, passing the bottle around while we tried to decide what to do and where to go. I had an idea in my mind that I'd been thinking on all through that flight from the Panhandle, but I wasn't ready to tell my partners about it. I'd been thinking about it after the woman, Hester, had made the mistake in the hotel room that had almost got me killed. But it wasn't her I was thinking about, it was another woman—a woman who went a long time back in my past, maybe six years, and who'd never really left my mind.

Chulo said, "Villa Union, it pretty *proximal* to us. Maybe we go there tonight, no? You know Villa Union, Weelson?"

Oh, yes, I knew Villa Union. That was the little Mexican town we'd holed up in, me and two other partners, some six years past, just right after this one foot I was riding with had lost us $4,000 in gold because he was scared of water.

He'd also lost a damn good horse, which was what had taken me and my other partner, Les Richter, to that rancho where I'd met the little senorita that had been in my mind for so long.

But it was not a time to think on such things. Now was a time to get moving, to get some food in our bellies, and to have a little rest and some good times.

We owed ourselves that after all we'd been through.

"Let's mount up," I said. "Villa Union is as good a place as any to lay over a couple of days while we decide what to do next."

We put the horses in a lope and headed for the little town. It was about six miles away, and we made that in just over an hour, even as tired as both we and our horses were. We came cantering on in, in good style, and I took note the little town hadn't changed that much in the years since I'd been there. It was mostly a collection of little adobe shacks with red-tile roofs. But they did still have a cantina with a few rooms to let and maybe some food a man could eat if he was hungry enough. They was the same bunch of peons sitting and laying around, watching us as we came cantering in, and the same bunch of chickens and goats and children running in the street. I reckon we looked a sight to them:

three big strangers wearing those big *pistoleros* and not appearing to care if the sun rose or set.

But we didn't pay no attention to them, just came up in front of the cantina, dismounted, tied our horses, and went on in, our big spurs jingling on the hard-packed dirt.

Well, they wasn't nobody in the place to speak of; a couple of old men sitting at a table in the back drinking tequila and playing *boleto*. One young *vaquero* at the bar, a fat bartender looking about half asleep, and a fat waitress that could have passed for the double of the one Tod had wanted to take to bed for ten pesos until we'd shamed him out of it.

We took up a table and the bartender came over. Chulo told him in Spanish we wanted a bottle of his best brandy, and it had better be the best else we was going to get a little bothered.

Not that we expected to get much in such a place, but he did come back with a bottle, wiping the dust off it with a rag, and it was brandy. Such as it was.

So we poured out all around and knocked them back for luck and then kind of settled back.

"Ahhh," Chulo said. "A long journey, eh, *amigos*?"

"*Seguro, como no?*" I told him. And Wilcey said, "You got that damn straight."

All of a sudden, sitting there in that same cantina, the past came flooding back on me. I didn't want it to, but it did anyway.

It had been those six years since I'd last been in Villa Union. That had been just after me and my two partners, the cousins Les and Tod Richter, had successfully robbed the bank in Carrizo Springs, only to lose the money in the Rio Grande, which was at flood stage, when Tod had lost his head because of his fear of water. Tod was about the worst fool I'd ever known, and if it hadn't been for his cousin,

Les, who was about the best man I've ever known, I wouldn't have put up with him until the water got hot.

Well, there we'd been in Villa Union, with very little money and a horse short. Me and Les had ridden out to this rancho, leaving Tod at the very same cantina me and my two partners were sitting in to try and get Tod a horse. Well, it had been an elegant place and the old Don a gentleman of the first water. We'd presented ourselves as cattle buyers and horse ranchers temporarily down on our luck and had managed to buy an old loose-gaited, long-necked traveling pony for Tod. But what had taken my heart was this brief encounter with the Don's niece, who was visiting him from her town of Sabinas Hidalgo. Her name was Linda and I'd carried the vision of that little highborn senorita in my breast for more years than I'd cared to remember.

After that had come the ill-fated robbery we'd tried on the bank in Uvalde. It had been my resolve to pull one more robbery to gain enough money to present myself in Sabinas Hidalgo as a man honestly looking to establish a horse ranch and to court that little Linda and win her for my wife. But the robbery at Uvalde had failed. Howland Thomas and his partner, Chico, had been killed on the spot, and Tod had been so badly wounded that he'd died on the way to the border. Only Les and I had crossed the Rio Grande safely. There we'd parted; him to go to Nuevo Laredo and me to go to Sabinas Hidalgo, for even as broke as I was, I determined to find some way to court that Linda senorita.

I had managed one dinner with her and her family and then word had come that Les lay near dying in Nuevo Laredo, shot by two bounty hunters. I had spurred my horse only to arrive too late, for he was dead already. I had very nearly gotten myself killed in an attempt to revenge him by killing the two bounty hunters. I had lived, but as shot up as

I was, it had been a near thing and had taken me months to recover.

After that I'd stayed on the jump, just barely ahead of the law, out of partners, unable to do any robbery of any consequence, and all the while carrying the vision of Linda inside me like an ache that couldn't be filled with anyone but her.

Then my business had turned fortunate and me and Chulo and a young man named Chauncey Jones, who was near as big a fool as Tod, had managed to successfully rob a train. Chauncey had been killed, but me and Chulo had got away to Mexico—even though Chulo had lost an eye—with better than $14,000 apiece in gold. I'd headed for Sabinas Hidalgo, sure now, with the money I had, that I could present myself as a reputable, honest man and woo Linda and win her.

She had been married just six weeks before I got there; married to the son of the president of the bank there in Hidalgo.

Well, it had been one of the hardest blows in my life. But there had been nothing for me to do but ride away in my pain and disappointment. Unfortunately, I'd been forced into a gunfight as I was leaving town, and I'd killed one of the *alcalde*'s council, which had made it pretty hot for me. After that I'd squatted in various border towns, ready to jump either way, depending on which law was the hottest after me. I'd done mostly gambling, which was where I'd run up on Wilcey and another gambler called Preacher after his habit of praying to the Lord, right in the middle of a poker game, to give him the winning hand.

We'd robbed a poker game in El Paso, went broke in California, ended up robbing that ranch in the Panhandle, where the Preacher had been killed, and now I was back in Mexico.

And all the time I'd carried the thought of that Linda with me, the memory of not having her like a sharp knife in my heart. I reckoned there hadn't been a day passed that my thoughts didn't somehow turn to her.

But somewhere along the line that longing I'd felt for her had gradually turned to bitterness for what she'd done to me. Now, if truth be told, she hadn't done nothing to me, but a man don't always control his feelings with his brain. I reckoned I was bitter that I couldn't have her, but the reason didn't make no never mind. Bitterness is bitterness and, for a time, I'd tried to take it out on other women. But that hadn't worked. They'd always ended up taking it out on me.

Hell, I'd never had no luck with women.

Nor with partners, for that matter. I'd lost Les and Tod. Then Chauncey Jones and then the Preacher. Never mind that he'd been killed in a poker game in the town of Tascosa, fifteen miles from where me and Wilcey had been holed up in a line camp. He'd still been my responsibility. He was not a gunman, but association with me had led him to believe he was, and I considered that my fault. I'd avenged his murder, but it still hadn't made me feel any better.

And now I had led my partners to Villa Union. I had led them there deliberately and with a plan in mind. There were maybe a hundred other crossings we could have made, but I'd headed straight for Villa Union for I knew what I was going to do. Presently I would tell them, but now was not the time. I knew my intentions would be dangerous for all concerned, but I didn't plan to lose any more partners. I was all done with that. And these two were good men; there wasn't a fool in the bunch. We'd be able to handle what might come our way.

Chulo, the black Mexican, was near as mean as he looked, and he was about the meanest-looking man I'd ever seen. He had a hooked nose and a knife scar down one cheek and a black patch over the eye he'd lost in the train robbery. He was also about the best man to have by your side in a tight that I've ever known. And me and him had been in our share of tight places.

Wilcey, like I said, I'd only known about four years, having met him in that poker game in Sanderson when he'd saved my bacon from three old boys who'd valued the money that was on my head more than they'd valued their lives. He reminded me a great deal of Les which, I reckon, was the reason I'd taken to him so quick. He didn't look much like Les, though they was both tall and slim. No, it was more his way of moving, more his way of saying things. It was me had led him into the life of an outlaw. He'd been a successful rancher until his wife had run off with another man, and then he'd taken to drink and gambling until he'd lost everything. When I'd met him he'd been getting by as a gambler, but not much more. I'd always felt a little bad about directing him along the owl hoot trail, but he'd said he wouldn't have it any other way. He was not of a class with a gun as Chulo and I were, but he was steady and cool and loyal to the bone. His only flaw was his bitterness toward women, all women. He'd said that he'd use women the rest of his life, but he was never again, by God, going to trust one. He was about of an age with me, thirty-four, though not as heavy nor as strong as I was at six feet one inch and one hundred and eighty pounds.

I never knew how old Chulo was. Hell, he could have been thirty or fifty for all I knew.

"What you thenk, Weelson?" Chulo said, breaking into my reverie.

"I thenk," I said, mocking his accent, "that we get plenty drunk, see if there is any *chiquitas* around here to fuck, rest a couple of days, and then I got a plan."

"What is it, Will?" Wilcey asked me.

I shook my head. "It ain't that well thought out, Dennis,"

I said. Dennis was Wilcey's first name, though I seldom called him that. "Let's just get drunk and see if something strikes me."

After a couple of drinks more we went out and led our horses down to this little livery stable and got them seen to and then we went back to the cantina and arranged for some rooms. Wilcey and I had taken one together and Chulo got him one. We'd brought our saddles and bedrolls back with us and I slung mine on the bed I was going to sleep on, figuring my own lice was better'n those of the man that had slept in the bed before me.

Wilcey was just sitting across the room on his bunk, a bottle of rum between his legs. He said, "Will, what you got in mind for us to do?"

I answered him kind of sharply. "Nothing, goddamnit! I told you I'd have a plan when the time come, but I ain't come down to that yet." I took my sleeve and wiped the sweat off my brow. It was dreadful hot, even inside them abode walls. "Hell," I said, "we're going to rob somebody. That's for sure. Because that's what we do for a living. I just ain't figured out who yet. Is that all right?"

He picked up the bottle of rum and took a drink, kind of wincing a little as it went down. "I reckon," he said. "But I been knowing you long enough to know you got something on your mind."

"I'd like to find something to fuck around here," I said. "I got that on my mind. But I doubt if they's a thing. Other'n that I ain't really studying about nothing except getting good and drunk and kind of resting from that ride we made. That and trying to evade any law that might be looking for us. Though I don't expect none in this here little *pueblo*."

He said, "All right. Then I reckon I was reading you wrong."

We ate a little supper, making do with beans and beef and

tortillas. Then we sat around drinking. Business never did pick up much, being mostly confined to a few townspeople and some sorry-looking sheepherders who mostly drank pulque, which was the cheapest thing available. I reckoned our custom, drinking what we were and throwing a little money around, was welcome. We just kept on sitting around, not saying much of anything. Every now and then my thoughts turned to this woman, Hester, whom I'd left in the hotel room in Amarillo with the law pouring through the door. But, more and more they were on Linda. I'd carried that woman too long in my heart and my head to just let her end as a memory. I hadn't gotten it straight yet, but I knew I was going to do something.

There wasn't a *puta*, a whore, in the town, but the waitress done a little side work on top of her duties in the cantina. After trade got slow enough, Chulo took her back in his room. She was just an ordinary, fat, greasy-haired Mexican woman with enough beads around her neck to have slowed a steer. I couldn't have stuck her, but Chulo, them white teeth flashing in his black face, said he didn't give a damn. "I have had the worst."

"Yeah," Wilcey said, "and you're liable to have the clap."

Chulo had laughed. "Oh, I got that now. *No le hace.*"

Which means it don't make no difference. Nothing makes any difference. But you got to be a Mexican to really understand what it means. I guess I'd always admired Chulo and his don't-give-a-damn attitude. Me. I'd always cared. I'd always worried. Chulo, if he had a woman and a bottle of whiskey and a little gold to jingle in his pocket through the night, truly didn't give a damn if the sun came up the next morning.

I'd drifted into the outlaw business when I was seventeen and then had spent the next seventeen years trying to get out of it. But, like I said, I'd been giving that a good deal of thought lately. I was about to get tired of fighting my head. It seemed like I was fated to be an outlaw and it began to seem that I ought to just quit trying to figure out a way to lead a decent life and give in to it. Hell, I was an outlaw. Seemed like I was made for it.

But not the killing. I can truthfully say I never killed a man except in defense of my life or that of one of my friends or when I was backed into a corner and given no selection. I never killed a cripple. I don't mean a cripple like someone who limps or ain't got but one arm. I mean a man who wouldn't have a chance against me. I've walked away from a lot of half-drunk kids in saloons, who didn't know what they were getting into, that I could have killed so quick they'd have never felt the lights go out. Or some cowboys who fancied themselves good with a gun because they could shoot rattlesnakes. No, I've turned my back on more fights than I've been in. You get a reputation as Wilson Young and you better figure on trouble wherever you go. And sometimes you got to be as good to avoid trouble as you do to end it. It was maybe the one fact in my whole sorry life that I could point to with any pride.

But I was starting to get tired of that. A man can hit himself in the head with his own bad feelings for just so long. There finally comes a day when pride revolts and mine was getting ready. All right, I'd robbed. But so had a lot of other people. They'd stolen, right after the Civil War, everything my daddy had spent fifty years in building up. Little by little they'd taken our ranch right outside of Corpus Christi until there wasn't nothing left. Only they hadn't done it with guns. They'd done it with Yankee lawyers and carpetbags full of them legal papers that hadn't got a goddamn thing to do with fairness. And they'd killed him just as sure as if they'd taken a gun and shot him in the breast.

So I was gaining on that place where Chulo lived. He never seemed to worry about a goddamn thing; not even the clap.

Wilcey said, "Will, why don't we fall off the trail awhile? Take a little time off?"

I shook my head. "We ain't got enough money for that. Little over $4,000 a man. Way we spend it that wouldn't last till the water got hot. Then we'd get desperate for money and pull some fool job that we wouldn't touch if we had time and leisure to check around. No, we got to do some more robbing."

"Texas or Mexico?"

I had my boots up on the table and I clinged my spurs together. "Oh, Mexico, of course," I said, trying to make a little joke out of it. "We got to be fair about this. Turn and turnabout. We done penetrated a deed in Texas. Now it's Mexico's turn. Hell."

It disturbed me fooling my partner like that, acting like I didn't know what I had in mind. But I couldn't do it alone. I needed them and what I had to do was figure out a way to draw them in without them realizing what I was really after.

It kind of made me feel dog dirty. But I couldn't do it by myself, and I had to do it or go on being haunted the rest of my life. Yet I vowed to myself I wouldn't lose a partner on the job. I didn't know how I'd accomplish that end, but I wouldn't. I'd lose my own life first.

I laid awake that night thinking. Over in the other bunk Wilcey was snoring lightly. We'd drunk considerable, but it didn't seem as if it had touched me. I knew I wouldn't rest until I'd figured out what to do.

Sometime before dawn I decided I couldn't make no plans so far away. The only thing to do was to go to Sabinas Hidalgo and scout out the situation and make plans from there. Of course this was a little complicated by the fact that

I'd killed the *alcalde*'s councilman the last time I'd been there, and they might be on the lookout for me. But I'd handle that situation when it came up.

I didn't say nothing the next day and we just went on the way we'd been doing—eating, drinking, and just kind of generally resting up. Chulo would go off with the waitress every so often and come back looking just as mean as ever. I'd wondered what a woman thought about going to bed with that vicious-looking sonofabitch. I bet they were scared not to do anything he wanted them to.

Me and Wilcey loafed around town a little. When the beggar kids got to plaguing us too bad, we'd sling a handful of coins out in the street and watch them flailing away. I sometimes wondered what those people in town thought of us, but you couldn't read nothing off their faces. But, then, I reckoned they'd seen gringo *pistoleros* before. Villa Union was a damn good town to hole up in.

At breakfast, on the morning of the third day, I finally come around to breaking it to them. We'd finished eating and was having a little rum to settle our stomachs. I said, "Well, it's about time to saddle up and get out of here."

Wilcey asked, quickly, "Where?"

I answered him softly, picking the way I wanted to say it. I said, "Well, it seems to me like we ought to get off the border to do any robbery. They going to be looking for us pretty hot around here. I know of a bank in a little town about one hundred miles south of here that's a real cracker box. I expect we ought to go down there and make a withdrawal. They ain't going to be looking for us that far south."

Wilcey said, "What town, Will?"

I said it casually. "Sabinas Hidalgo."

The black Mexican said, cheerfully, "Ah, I know that *chiquita puebla*. Is *muy bueno*."

But Wilcey wasn't listening to Chulo. He was staring hard at me. He asked me, softly, "Will, have you forgot all them talks we had in that line camp when we was waiting to rob that ranch payroll?"

I looked at him, reading in his eyes what he was getting at. "No," I said, "I ain't forgot. What are you driving at?"

He said, "They's a hundred little towns in Mexico with banks. Why Sabinas Hidalgo?"

"Why not?" I challenged him.

"I know," he said.

"Then if you know, tell me."

TWO

Wilcey said, "It's because of that girl, that girl Linda."

"I'll be goddamn if that's so!" I said, getting angry because I was lying. I'd never lied to partners before.

"Yes, it is," he said, looking at me steadily.

"Goddamnit, Wilcey!" I said, flaring up. "Don't you goddamn well say something like that to me."

Chulo said, "What is this talk you are making? *Que dices?*"

Wilcey didn't turn his head to Chulo, just kept looking at me. "Wilson's fixing to get us in a storm over some goddamn woman he's been dreaming about for years."

Well, I guess I'd mentioned Linda to Chulo back in San Antonio, back when I was sleeping with his cousin's sister, just before we pulled the train robbery, but if he'd heard me he'd long since forgotten. So he just shrugged and said, "Trouble is trouble. For the reason is not so *importa.*"

"Listen, Wilcey," I said, "just watch that kind of talk."

"You want to tell me it ain't true?"

"What ain't true?"

"That we're heading for Hidalgo because of that Linda girl. That you didn't decide that was the bank to rob because of her. Didn't you tell me her husband is the son of the president of that selfsame bank?"

I got up stiffly. "Listen," I said, "we can come to a fork in the trail right now if you feel like that. Ain't nothing says you got to come with me." I was mad at myself for lying, but I was even madder at getting caught at it. "And Chulo ain't got to come neither," I said.

But Wilcey just shook his head. "No, I'm coming. You know that. I just wish you'd tell me the straight of it. That's all."

"The hell with you," I said. I turned around and walked back to the little room and started gathering my gear up. In a few minutes Wilcey came in, but he didn't say nothing. After I had my gear ready to travel, I went down and ordered up enough grub for all of us for what I figured would be a three-day trip, if we took it easy and I didn't see no reason to rush. I also got a half-dozen bottles of rum off the bartender. Then I went down to the livery stable, settled my score, and led my horse back to the front of the cantina. When I went in to get my gear out of the room, Wilcey was sitting on the side of his bunk nipping out of a rum bottle. "Are we about ready to take out?" he asked me carefully.

I looked at him. "If you're going. At least I am."

He give me that little half-cynical lopsided grin of his. "Was I out of line, Will?"

"Damn right," I said. "That was a hell of a thing to say to a partner."

"Maybe," he said. Then he asked me if I'd arranged for grub yet.

"Yes."

"For all of us?"

"Oh, go to hell, Wilcey," I said. I gathered up my gear and went outside and began packing it aboard. Chulo was already doing the same. *"Que pasa, amigo?"* he said cheerfully.

"Nada." I was still feeling pretty bad. Hell, I should have told them what I had in mind from the first. They might not have gone for it, but at least I'd of felt better.

We trailed out in early afternoon, heading out of town on a southeasterly direction, going through the baking prairie full of rocks and cactus and stunted mesquite trees. It was plenty hot. We might have done better to wait for evening, but I was eager to get going. I was mounted on a good bay gelding that I'd been riding for better than two years. He was iron hard, a real stayer, but with plenty of early speed. One thing men in our profession have got to have the best of and that's guns and horses. My two partners were as well mounted as I was. It don't do no good for two of a three-man party to be riding good horses if the third is on a mount that's inferior to the other two for, unless you are willing to run off and leave a partner, your speed and stamina is going to be dragged down to what his horse can do.

It was going to be a long hot ride. Sweating, and taking off my hat to wipe the sweat off my brow, it was hard to believe that not three months past, December of 1895, we'd been in some serious danger of freezing up in the Panhandle. It was early 1896, but now it was hard to believe we'd ever been that cold.

We kept on through the afternoon, taking it slow, stopping to rest our horses every little while, and then on through early evening. Just before it commenced to become really dark, I selected us a camping place and we made our stop for the night. It didn't actually matter where we stopped, for the country was pretty much the same—just rolling prairie covered with cactus and weeds and not a tree in sight except, here and now, a stunted mesquite that didn't throw enough shade to cool off a small goat. We would have to make a dry camp. To the best of my memory we wouldn't strike water until sometime the next day. Until then we'd have to make do with what we had. But we were all right; we had plenty of grub and grain for the horses and enough water for ourselves and a little for the horses.

Chulo got a fire going and we made coffee and then warmed up the beans and beef we'd brought. The sun had gone down and it was starting to cool off. We sat around the fire, racked up against our saddles, and took a plate of grub and ate. Our horses were picketed on long ropes where they could get plenty of grass. We'd given them a little drink of water before turning them out, and they'd be all right until we could get to good water the next day.

Wilcey hadn't had much to say to me since we'd finished our conversation in the room. Every once in a while he'd give me that little lopsided grin like he was telling me he knew what I was about and why didn't I go ahead and own up to it.

Hell, all that done was piss me off.

"Ah," Chulo said, when we'd finished eating, *"es bueno."*

"You ought to feel all right, you damn *Meskin,"* I told him. "You've spent two days wallowing around in that damn *puta,* and filling your belly with whiskey and food. Goddamn *chingale* like you don't need no better."

He looked over at me. *"Como no, senor?"*

As if to say, "What more can a man want?"

But Wilcey said, "Tell us about that bank in Hidalgo, Will?"

Well, truth be told I didn't know a goddamn thing about

that bank, except what I'd observed from riding by it. But I was damned if I'd give Wilcey the satisfaction of catching me out on so lazy a play.

I said, "Ain't much to tell. Just one big room. Couple of teller windows up front. President's got him a little desk at back. Ya'll go in and get the money while I tend to anyone that wants to interfere. Be mostly gold."

Wilcey said, "Sounds like about every other bank in every other small town in Mexico. What makes this one so special?"

I looked over at him. "Goddamnit, Wilcey," I said, a little heat in my voice. "You better watch yourself." I knew what he was doing.

"Hell, I'm just asking a question. Man goes to rob a bank he's got a right to know what to expect."

"Don't give me that shit," I said.

But he was looking squarely back, the flickers from the fire making shadows dance across his face. "What shit, Will? What are you talking about?"

"Go to hell," I said. I got up and got me a handful of sand and commenced to scour out my tin plate. Then I put it in my saddlebags and went to where I'd spread my bedroll out and lay down. I said, "We need to get after it early. Stay out of the heat. We'll hole up in the afternoon at the water hole I know about."

Then I took my boots off and lay back down and shut my eyes.

We got out before light next morning, making do for breakfast with coffee and cold beef and tortillas.

Chulo said, "Aiee, I feel more safe to be in Mexico. The law is much worse here." Then he laughed.

But Wilcey said, "Yeah, but they still carry guns and shoot real bullets."

"But not so well, I thenk," Chulo said.

It was hot almost as soon as the sun got up. One thing for
sure, there was going to be damn little drinking with this
heat. Once, about midmorning, I took out a bottle of rum
and uncorked it and raised it to my mouth and the fumes that
had built up damn near knocked me out. I just shoved the
cork back in and replaced it.

We went along, slogging through the hot sun, every now
and then calling a rest. About two of the afternoon we
finally sighted the watering hole that I'd remembered. It was
a big, spring-fed stock tank, and we came slogging down to
it glad for the rest for ourselves and our horses.

We hadn't made a nooning so we set up a campfire and
heated the beans and the beef and the tortillas while our
horses, glad to be free of their saddles, rolled on their backs
in the mud at the edge of the water.

Sitting back, eating, Chulo asked me, "How much *dinero*
you thenk we get out of this *Meskin* bank, *amigo?*"

"I don't know," I said, very conscious of Wilcey's eyes on
me. *"Quine sabe?"* Who knows. I added, "Enough."

Wilcey asked, "And then what, Will? Where do we go
from there?"

"I don't know," I said. "My thinking right now is that we
might hit southeast for the coast. Maybe go to Vera Cruz or
somewhere down in there. They ain't going to be looking
for us in such a place. *You* got any better ideas?"

He shook his head. "No. You're running the show."

I got a tin cup and poured me out a little luke-warm water
in it and then added a little rum. Then I offered the bottle
around, but no one wanted any. It was all I could do to sip
the hot mixture down and keep it down. But, once it had
settled in my belly, I began to feel somewhat better.

We filled up on water the next morning and then left out
early. About midmorning we passed the tiny village of
Guzman. Chulo wanted to go in and see if they had a

cantina, but I said no. I didn't want nobody seeing us nor any word of our coming being passed around.

While I was riding, I thought that my plan to hit the bank and then head for the coast was a sound one. It would have been just about perfect if it hadn't of been for my own private intentions. And, of course, our plans for robbing a bank would have been a lot better if it hadn't of been the bank in Hidalgo I'd chosen.

But, no matter, my mind was made up.

In early afternoon we topped a little rise and the town of Sabinas Hidalgo lay spread out in the valley floor before us. It was a pretty little town, prettier than I'd remembered; whitewashed adobe buildings with red-tile roofs. Neat streets, carefully laid out. And all around the town the green of the fields.

"There it be," I said.

Chulo wanted to know where the bank was. The town was built around a central plaza, and I pointed to a large, stone building on the upper righthand side of the street across from the square. Next door to it was the hotel I'd stayed at while I'd made my careful plans to go and court Linda. "Right there," I said. "That two-story building. Don't know if you can see from here, but it's the one with iron bars over the windows."

Wilcey said, "Don't look like no cracker box to me."

I said quickly, "We ain't going in by the window."

We stood looking and then Chulo said, "Pronto! Why do we wait? Let us do the promenade into town and taste the quality of their wheesky and weemen."

I shook my head. "No, chico. I can't go into that town. Not just yet. A few years back I killed an important politico and I fear they would remember me. No, we have to make a camp back up here and then Wilcey and you can go in."

The land, in the little valley, was lush with greenery and

water, and it wasn't long before we found a little creek bed, about two miles out of town, with a thin trickle of water running down it. There was good grass for the horses and there were some hanging willows for shade. It wasn't very well fortified, the banks of the creeks being too shallow to make good cover, but it was a good, cool camp. Besides that, I didn't see where we were going to need to fort up on this particular job.

We got unloaded and set up and then I told Chulo and Wilcey to go on into town and look around. "I reckon," I said, looking up at the sun, "that the bank's already closed. But you might just kind of hang around and get the lay of the land."

Wilcey give me a kind of a funny look, but they went ahead and went into town. After they were gone I got me a tin cup, got some of that cool creek water, and mixed me up a drink with the rum. Then I sat back down against my saddle and sat there cooling out after the hard ride. It was still plenty hot, but the little shady place down by the creek wasn't so bad. I sat there smoking and drinking and trying not to do too much thinking. It wasn't time for thinking yet, especially the kind of thinking I was going to have to do.

I was expecting them to be gone the balance of the day and well into the night. Way we'd been running I figured they'd treat themselves to a little good times. But it wasn't two hours before Wilcey rode back into the camp. He unsaddled and staked his horse and came over and helped himself to a little of the rum.

"Where's Chulo?" I asked him.

"He stayed in town. Figures to get drunk and go to the whorehouse."

"Why did you come back?"

"Aw, I don't know." He sipped at his whiskey. "Just wasn't ready. Might go back when it gets cooler."

We was silent for a few minutes and then Wilcey said, "Will, I don't get it. Tell me how you're going to plan a bank robbery without going in and looking over the layout?"

"Oh, I'm going in," I said. "I just figured to let you and Chulo get the lay of the land before I did. Find out about the local law, get some idea of who's around town. I'm going in, I'm just not going to make no habit of it."

He walked down to the creek, filled his tin cup again, and then added rum. When he sat back down he said, "We got into that bank. It was still open."

"Oh, yeah? What'd it look like?"

He shrugged. "About like most of them I've seen. Looks like they might have a little cabbage in there. Got one guard. Old man with a carbine looks like it ain't been fired in ten years. He was about asleep in a chair when we walked in."

He was sitting sideways to me, not looking my way. He said, "President of that bank don't look like he could have any kids much out of diapers."

"Maybe it's the son," I said. "Maybe the old man died or retired."

"What's this Linda's new name? I mean, what would her husband's name be?"

I said, lying, "I'm not sure. Bustamante, I think." I was lying because I knew damn well what it was, but I didn't want Wilcey to know how long and hard it had been on my mind.

"That's the hombre," he said. "Don Eduardo Bustamante."

"What's he look like?"

Wilcey shrugged. "Oh, quality, I reckon. Pretty small. Got long sideburns and slicked back hair and a neat little mustache. Well dressed as you'd expect."

I sat there, visualizing the picture Wilcey had give me of the man that was sleeping in bed with the woman I'd been in love with so long. It was not a pleasant way of thinking, and I eventually wrenched my mind around. I said, "How much law you see in town?"

He said, "Didn't see any. Of course that don't mean they ain't plenty, but the place seems mighty quiet. I'm thinking," he went on, "that that ought to be a pretty easy bank to rob." Then he looked over at me. "That is, if that's all we're planning. Just to rob the bank and hit it for Vera Cruz."

"Aw, don't start that again, Wilcey. You seem determined to see if you can get me hot."

"No," he said. "I'm just trying to figure out what you got in mind."

"I done told you," I said, saying it steady and hard. "And I'm getting a little tired of your doubting me. You going back into town?"

"I thought I would," he said.

The sun was getting low, its bottom edge just about to touch the horizon. "Well, you and Chulo stay separated. In fact don't even act like you know each other. Ain't no use in nobody figuring out we're a gang. I'm going to stay out here tonight and go in tomorrow. Y'all might see if you can bring back a few bottles of decent whiskey or brandy. This rum is all right if you haven't got anything else." I got up and went down to the creek and got me a drink of straight water. I don't know what it is about rum, but it damn sure makes your mouth dry.

Wilcey rode out just as it come dark and it wasn't long before I was in my sleeping bag. Dark, it was good and cool, and I lay there staring up at the sky for a time. But I was tired and it wasn't long before I was asleep.

THREE

❧

Chulo came riding in just about the time me and Wilcey was making a breakfast of coffee and beef and tortillas. He swung down, looking tired but pretty content. After he'd seen to his horse, he hunkered down and took a cup of coffee and rum with us.

"How'd she go, *amigo*?" I asked him. "You get all them *putas* in town taken care of?"

He gave me a flash of white teeth, made whiter by the condition of his beard growth, which was a little blacker than the ace of spades.

"Ahhh," was all he said. He finished his coffee and said, "I thin' I go esleepe now."

"I'll bet," Wilcey said. "He was just getting warmed up when I left late last night."

Chulo went and rolled up in his blankets and went to sleep. Wilcey and I doused the fire and straightened up the camp, then I got me some water out of the creek and commenced to clean myself up as best I could. I didn't bother to heat water to shave, just made do with the cold as best I could.

Wilcey asked me, "You going in?"

"Thought I would," I said.

"Ain't that a little risky?"

"I don't know," I said. "I kind of thought I was in the risk-taking business as it was."

"Still," he said.

"I doubt they'll remember me. Been a few years back. At least four or five. Besides, all greasers look alike to gringos. Don't you reckon all gringos look alike to *Meskins*?"

"You going in the bank?"

"That's what we're going to rob, ain't it?"

I got my shirt back on, then caught my horse up and got him saddled. Then I climbed on board and told Wilcey, "I'll probably be back about early afternoon, siesta time."

"I'm going to trail in myself in a little while."

"All right. But don't act like you know me."

"You told me that yesterday," he said, a little edge in his voice.

Well, Wilcey was obviously being bothered by this job, jumpy as he was getting. Which wasn't like him at all. Truth to tell I was a little edgy myself.

On the short ride in I could feel myself tensing up. It had been a long time since I'd been in Sabinas Hidalgo, and the last time I'd left it had been one of the heart breakingest times I'd ever been through. I could feel my chest and throat tighten as I realized I was riding into the very town where Linda was and that I might, by accident, see her that very day.

It was a strange feeling after all the time that had passed. I wondered if she was still as beautiful as she had been. In the years that had passed she might have commenced to have kids and gotten fat. Mexican women do that after they get married and settle down. Church laws don't let them get split up, so once they've got their man, they don't make no effort about themselves no more.

But, somehow, I just couldn't see Linda doing that. For her to get ugly would be the same thing as a bird forgetting how to fly.

Then, all too soon, I was cantering up a street into the main plaza of the town. I couldn't remember it well enough to know if it had changed. It was still one of the cleanest Mexican towns I'd been in, all whitewashed buildings and red-tiled roofs. The plaza was still as it had been, shade trees all around the sides and benches and a bandstand in the middle. It was on that very plaza that I'd stood, hidden by a tree, and watched Linda and her sisters one Sunday taking the promenade, the young bucks of the town walking in the opposite direction, each eyeing the other while the chaperones looked on to see that no foolishness got started. Likely her present husband had been one of them young bucks that Sunday.

Of course it had been right after that that I'd got the telegram about Les being shot, and I'd had to make a run for Nuevo Laredo.

I pulled my horse up in front of the hotel where I'd stayed before, the hotel where I'd run into the drunk I'd killed, the mayor's councilman. I tied my horse and then went on into the bar. It was about ten of the morning, but the place was open though they wasn't doing much custom. There were a couple of quality-looking hombres having their midmorning coffee and talking, as Mexicans will, very excitedly and using their hands a lot.

I sat down at a table. The bartender, who'd been dozing against the wall behind the bar, looked up and I ordered cognac. He brought it over and then went back behind the bar. Nobody was paying me the slightest bit of attention.

I sat there sipping at the good cognac, trying to decide what I ought to do. Obviously, the two important things to do were to find out where Linda and her husband lived and to have a look at the bank.

I had a couple of more drinks, just sitting there thinking. A few hombres wandered in and out. They glanced my way, but no more than what you'd do with any casual stranger.

Finally I got up and wandered out on the street. It wasn't hard to find the bank. I went and stood in front of it. It was fixing to come noon and traffic on the street was running pretty slow. Finally I mounted the little steps and went on in. The front door was a heavy affair with just a little piece of glass in it and iron bars over that. The inside was cool and dark. I stopped just inside the door to sort of give the place a pretty good looking over. It looked about average, long and kind of narrow. The teller cages were on the left with a few desks in the back and some little tables to the right. The guard was sitting there, his carbine propped across his knees. In the direct back was the vault. The door was standing open, but I didn't care about that. The plan I was starting to get in mind, they'd open that vault whether they wanted to or not. Maybe even bring us the gold.

The guard kind of looked up while I stood there, but then he went back to staring at the far wall. I sauntered up to one of the teller cages and pitched a double eagle down and asked for change for it in pesos. The clerk was a neat-looking little man wearing a high collar. While he counted out the paper money, I took a careful look at the bank. There was one big desk with nobody at it, and that's where I figured my soon-to-be *amigo*, Linda's husband, hung his hat. I kept stalling, hoping he'd show up while I was still there so I could get a look at him. To do that I protested that the clerk was giving me too many small bills and that they would not fit in my pocket.

"*Perdoneme,* senor," he said, and swept all the money up and began laying out a new set.

About that time a man came out of the vault and settled himself behind the desk. Wasn't the slightest bit of doubt in my mind that that was the package I was looking for. Oh, he was a careful-looking number all right. All done up in a business suit with them long sideburns and that neat little mustache and that slicked-back hair. He sat there at his desk, going over some papers, while I watched him.

If he could have known what I was thinking, I reckon he wouldn't have looked so smug.

Not unless he was awful brave. And he damn sure didn't look that way to me.

Well, I was staying too long and I knew it. Finally, I shoved the money down in my pocket, took one more look around, and then sauntered on out. Outside, I glanced up and down the street. It was still pretty slow.

From my past visit I knew there was an outpost of Mexican soldiers, the *Federales,* stationed toward the south edge of town. I walked that way, wondering if they were still there. A lot of the bandit trouble had moved on to the north and the *Federales* had moved with them.

I walked down the dusty street, just kind of taking it all in. There were four roads leading off the plaza, all of them going in pretty much different directions. One thing I liked about the layout was the town was pretty bunched up, meaning that if we could make our getaway from the central part, we'd be out in the country and running and any catch party coming after us would have to take us on amidst open ground.

I kept walking away from the plaza for a good three or four hundred yards until I came to where the *Federales*'s

barracks had once been. They were still there all right.
There was a little guard house out front. I walked to the door
of that, and there was a sergeant sitting there with his feet up
on the desk reading a periodical. I looked in and waited for
him to look up. When he did he said, *"Monday?"*

"Nada," I said, and turned. He'd looked pretty well like
there wasn't much authority left around; looked like he was
just biding his time until somebody came and relieved him.

That was all right. In fact it was better than I'd expected.

I walked back downtown, my spurs jingling from the hard
ground. There were a number of *ninos* lounging around in
front of the hotel, and I picked me out a bright-looking boy
of about twelve, wearing white britches tied at the ankles
and a straw sombrero. In Spanish I asked him, *"Usted
conoce la casa del presidente del banco?"*

He said, *"Si, como no?"*

I pitched him a twenty-five-centavo piece and told him to
lead me there, only wait until I got my horse. Then I
mounted up, and with him leading the way, running in front
of me, his *huarachas* throwing up little puffs of dust from
the dry streets, we started out of town.

We didn't go far. After we passed the last outskirts of the
town buildings, he pulled up and pointed at a large house
sitting on a wide open section of prairie.

"Esta," he said. *"Es la casa del senor presidente del
banco Bustamante."*

I pitched him another coin and then sat there looking. It
was a big house, but it was obviously still a building. It was
not a rancho, not a place where a man raised cattle or horses.
It was a rich man's house, the kind of house that a man
might begin building if he'd just become the president of his
daddy's bank.

I urged my horse forward until I was standing in the road
in front of it.

I sat there looking at it, knowing that Linda was probably somewhere inside and knowing that within a few days I'd be in there with her.

Me and her husband.

I sat a long few minutes, remembering a lot of things, remembering a lot of nights around a lot of campfires, remembering a lot of nights in a lot of hotel rooms. Remembering a lot of hours that I'd spent thinking of her.

Well, I was going to get her out of my heart once and for all.

I turned my horse and rode slowly back to the hotel, thinking a lot of thoughts a man shouldn't think. It had come the siesta time as I dismounted and went into the hotel and the street was even quieter than before. I half expected the bar to be closed, but that was not the case. I went in and took a table and ordered another cognac. There was only one other patron in the place, a small, sharp-featured, well-dressed man sitting at a table by himself in the corner. He glanced at me as I came in, but I paid him no mind, just sat down and took my drink from the bartender and began sipping at it, deep in my own thoughts.

I don't know how much time passed, maybe ten minutes, and then I became aware of this hombre standing at my table. I glanced up. It was the sharp-featured little gent from the back table, I'd had my boots propped in an adjoining chair and I slowly set them on the floor and straightened up.

"Yeah?" I asked him.

"I would speak with you," he said. He talked English, but with a pretty good Mexican accent. "Would you permit me to sit down?"

"Help yourself," I said, watching him carefully. I glanced quickly around the room. We were still the only customers in the place and the bartender continued to doze against the far wall. I shoved a chair out for him with my boot and he sat down, mopping his brow with a fine silk handkerchief.

"Have a drink," I offered, it being the custom of the country to be polite, whether you felt like it or not.

He tucked his handkerchief back in his pocket and declined. "Thank you, no, senor. I have just had a coffee."

I said, "Well, what can I do for you?"

He looked at me for a second, looking like he was trying to figure out how to say something. Then he said, "I think you have been in Sabinas Hidalgo before."

I looked at him carefully. "I might have ridden through before," I said. "Why?"

"No, that is not my meaning." He was looking a little nervous, which was making me nervous. "I think you were here for several days some few years back."

"I get around a lot," I said carefully. I wasn't liking the way the conversation was going. "Is it any of your business?"

"Perhaps," he said. He got out his handkerchief and wiped his brow off again. "Is very hot," he said.

I said, "And it might get hotter."

He took my meaning in a hurry and commenced to get worried. "Oh, no, no, no, senor. I am not here for to make you trouble. No, the contrary. If you are the gentleman I believe you to be. Then I am here as in your debt."

Now this gent was starting to worry me seriously. I said, "I don't know who you think I am, but I ain't. I'm a stranger here and I intend to keep it that way."

But he had his teeth into something and he was determined to hang on. He said, "I am Joaquin Martin. There was a gringo gentleman shot a political rival of mine some several years back. I witnessed this timely deed. I believe you are the man."

Well, I just kind of pushed my chair back, getting my side, which bore my gun well clear. I said, mildly, "That's pretty serious talk. You sure you want to go on talking like that?"

He went at his brow with the handkerchief again, but he wouldn't give up on it. "Please senor, please understand I mean you no danger. You did me a great service in affecting the death of my political rival. I have approached you because I have a business proposition for you along the lines of your, uh, previous work."

I called to the bartender to give me my score. Then I got out the money and laid it on the table and stood up. "Mister," I said, "I don't know who the hell you are, or what you're up to. But I'm going to leave and, right now, that makes you the luckiest man in town."

He started to protest, but I just turned on my heel and walked out. Outside, I turned and watched the door of the hotel, but he didn't follow. Finally I mounted up and rode slowly out of town, glancing back every so often to be sure I wasn't followed.

It was midday when I got back to camp. Neither of my partners were there so I made myself a drink of whiskey and water and sat down to think things over. The visit from the little sharp-faced Mexican gentleman had left me a bit disturbed.

Chulo and Wilcey rode in just before dusk. I'd built a fire and was heating some of the beef we still had. They tended to their horses and then came up to the fire and squatted and got a drink of whiskey.

"Well, what have you two hombres been up to?"

Wilcey said, "I played a little cards." He jerked his finger at Chulo. "The Mex is still making up for lost time at the whorehouse."

I shook my head. "You going to wear them girls out, Nigger."

But my mood was not light. I was still worried about what

had happened in the bar. I had been thinking and thinking about what it might do to our plans. I had also been trying to decide if I should tell my partners.

Finally I said, "I think a man recognized me in the bar today."

They both turned to look at me, but didn't say anything. "Yeah," I said. I got a handful of the gravelly sand and let it run out of my palm. "I tried to bluff it out, but I don't think it worked."

"Do we need to make tracks?" Wilcey asked me.

"I don't know," I said. And I didn't. I explained to them what had happened. "So you see, I don't know if he's trouble or help."

Wilcey asked me, sounding puzzled, "What do you reckon he meant about having a job for you in your line of work?"

"Beats the hell out of me," I said. Then I laughed. "Unless he's got another political rival he wants killed."

"That's what it sounds like."

I picked up another handful of sand. "Not exactly my style."

Then we were silent for a few minutes, each of us lost in the news that I'd brought them. Wilcey asked me, "Will, what do we do?"

I took a long time answering him. I let another handful of sand run through my fingers. Then I said, "Chulo?"

He looked at me expectantly.

I said, "Listen, Nigger, I want you to go in and bring that sonofabitch out here to me tomorrow."

Wilcey said, "What are you talking about? You going to get us all killed."

But I was looking at Chulo. "His name is Joaquin Martin. He's some kind of *jefe* politician in town. I want you to go in tomorrow, find him, and bring him out here. Whether he wants to come or not."

Chulo just nodded. *"Si. Como no."* Why not.

To him it was simple and direct. But Wilcey said, "Will, have you lost your mind? You can't send Chulo in to just bring a man back. You'll have a hornet's nest down around our ears."

I ignored him. I said to Chulo, "He's a little sharp-featured man around forty. I think he takes his coffee of a morning in the bar of the hotel. Don't attract any attention. Just bring him along. I want him back here by noon tomorrow."

Chulo just shrugged. *"No es dificil."*

Wilcey said, "Oh shit, Will. You can't do this."

I turned around and looked at him. "Listen, partner," I said, "if this is going to bother you, you got some much rougher trails coming up down the road. You been about half right about what you've suspected about this job. It's going to get worse. If you haven't got the stomach for it, I recommend you get out right now."

"What are you saying?"

"You heard me. If you think me dragging some little politico out here is bad, you just wait and see what's coming next. The only thing I promise you is that we're going to get out of here with a lot of money and ain't either you, me, or Chulo going to get killed. Not if you do what I say. I been running this outfit ever since you joined up. And if you don't like them terms, then I reckon you better saddle your horse and ride out. You been in my face pretty bad this last few days. Ain't nothing keeping you here and I'm about to get tired of your doubting Thomas ways."

Well, it hit him. But it hit me, too. He looked over at me and then he leaned down and looked between his boots. Thinking. Studying on the matter. I knew my words had been harsh to him, but they'd had to been said. I couldn't go on with him mistrusting me as he was.

But I knew, while he was studying the ground between his boots, that if I lost Wilcey, I'd have lost my right arm. I knew that if he got up, which I was expecting him to do, and rode out I would have lost my best friend.

But I didn't know anything else to say. When you're running the dangerous kind of business we were running, you don't have the time to sit down and discuss all your plans. Somebody's got to be the boss and I was the boss of the outfit.

That's the way it had to be. And if Wilcey couldn't understand that, then we were going to have to lose him.

It was Chulo that saved the situation. He suddenly laughed and said to Wilcey, "Senor, is no *importa*. I have been with Weelson on many jobs and he has never gotten me killed. Only this." He flicked his eye patch and laughed again. "But that is not important. After all I have two eyes and what is one eye between friends. No, I think it would be unwise to worry about what Weelson thenks would be best." Then he looked over at me and pulled at his eye patch. "Is he not the *jefe?* The boss?"

After a long moment Wilcey lifted his eyes from between his boots and looked over at me. Then he looked at Chulo and then back at me. He said, "Will, I believe in you because you're all I've got to believe in now. Whatever you think suits me."

Hell, I didn't know what to say. Finally I just kind of cleared my throat and said, gruffly. "Well, that's all right. Now I reckon we all ought to get a little sleep. I want Chulo in early, looking that Martin fellow up. Let's hit the blankets."

I tossed and turned that night. Sometime, judging by the position of the moon, a few hours before dawn, I rolled out of my blankets and sat up. I was considerably bothered by what I was doing to my partners and I knew I had to tell them the truth. Or, rather, I had to tell Wilcey the truth. Chulo didn't give a damn either way.

So I got up and pulled on my boots and went over to where Wilcey was asleep in his bedroll. I shook him gently. When he opened his eyes, I cautioned him to be quiet. "I want to talk a bit," I said.

"What the hell," he said. But he rolled over and sat up. "Hell, when's morning?"

"Beats the hell out of me," I said. Let's walk off a bit so as not to wake Chulo up."

"All right."

He got up and followed me as I walked a bit off into the dark from our dying campfire. The ground sloped up from the creek, and I found us a place to sit on a rock ledge that had come cropping out of the ground. Wilcey was right behind me. I sat down and he took a seat a few feet away. For a long moment I didn't say anything, just got out one of them Mexican cigarillos I sometimes smoke, struck a phosphorus match on my boot, got my cigarillo lit, and sat there puffing for a minute.

Wilcey finally asked me, "What the hell's going on?"

I took a long time answering him. When I did I said, "Well, I guess I'm going to have to tell you the straight about this job. You've guessed most of it already, but I reckon I better lay it out all the way for you. Then if you want to ride out, I sure as hell won't blame you."

He said, "All right."

I knew I had to talk about it, but it was kind of hard to get the words out. It ain't easy to lie to your partners, but it's harder when you finally want to own up to the truth. I said, "It's true what you thought about why we're in Sabinas Hidalgo. It's that girl. That Linda. You were dead on it when you asked me why I'd picked this one Mexican town out of all the others to rob a bank in. It's because of her."

He waited, thinking I was going to go on, but I had stopped. Finally he said, "All right. What else?"

I drew on my cigarillo. "Nothing. Except I got to get her out of my mind. She's been there too long. And I got to see her one more time. That's the only way I know of."

He said, "All right. Then why don't you just ride up to her door and say hello?"

I shook my head. "Can't work that way. She don't know I exist. She hasn't been thinking of me all these years like I been thinking of her. I intend to get her attention."

"What does that mean?"

"I don't know yet," I said. I drew on my cigarillo, studying the glow it made in the dark. Finally I flipped it away, watching it make an arc through the air and then spark against the ground. "All I can tell you," I said, "is that when we leave this town she's going to know that Wilson Young is alive. I ain't going to keep her as a dream in my head anymore. I'm going to be flesh and blood to her and she's going to be flesh and blood to me."

What I'd just said hung there in the night for a long moment and then Wilcey said, "Are you saying what I think you're saying?"

"Yes," I said.

"What about the bank?"

"That, too," I answered. "That little greaser she married. I'm leaving this town with everything." I looked at him and my voice suddenly got hard. "And I mean everything. You understand me?"

He was a long time in answering. Around us the night was making quiet noises. He said, "Is it so serious with you?"

"Yes," I said. "And if I have to I'll do it on my own. I

can't go on with her following me around like a damn ghost.
For about six years I've been in love with a damn woman
that I've never so much as kissed. I touched her hand once."
I looked down at the dark ground. "I got to get shut of her."

He asked me, "You know how you're going to do it yet?"

I shook my head. "No. I got an idea, but I ain't got all the
details worked out. I got a feeling that this fellow Martin is
going to be a help, but I ain't sure." I got another cigarillo
and lit it, the match making a big flash in front of my face
in the night. When it was going good I said, "Only thing I
can promise is that I won't get neither you nor Chulo off in
no storm."

And then there was a long silence.

I waited, wondering what he'd have to say. At length he
said, "Is this the way it has to be?"

"Yes," I said. I was trying to keep back as much as I
could, for there's things a man don't want to tell another
man. But some of it spilled out. My voice got down low and
grating. I said, "Listen, that goddamn woman's been a
dream to me for so many years I don't want to think about
it. I can't count the nights I've tossed and tumbled and
thought about her. Only way I can ever get her out of my
head is to just treat her like a goddamn woman instead of the
ghost she is. So that's what I'm going to do. And I won't
blame you if you pull out."

I could barely see him in the dark, just see the profile of
his head and shoulders. He said, "Wish I had a drink."

"Myself."

He got up and went over to where my saddlebags were
laying and came back with a bottle of cognac. With his teeth
he pulled out the cork, took a pull, and then pitched it over
to me. I took a drink. It was pretty good French cognac. It
burned going down, but then it turned warm and some of the
pain went out of my belly.

Wilcey said, "I'm going back and get some sleep."

"What do you think?" I asked him.

He was about to walk off and he stopped and looked back at me. "About what?"

"About what I've told you."

"Why, it's all right."

"What does that mean?"

He was postured against the horizon and I could see him against the lighter sky. He raised and dropped his shoulders. "I mean, it's all right. Me and Chulo done talked about it. We know you're out of your goddamn mind, but ain't nothing we can do except try and get you straightened up. If this is what you've got to do, then we're in."

I said it lowly. I said, "Okay. Appreciate it."

I couldn't see his face in the dark, but I could imagine that sardonic smile. He said, "Hell, you're the *jefe*, ain't you? The boss?"

"Go to hell," I said.

He laughed and turned away to walk back to his blankets and a little sleep. I sat there staring at the glowing end of my cigarillo wondering why I was lucky enough to have such friends.

In the morning I asked Chulo if he had it all straight.

"*Si, que no,*" he said, shrugging. "Why not. *No es dificil.*"

"How you going to do it? What are you going to tell him to get him to come?"

He shrugged again. "*Yo no se.* I will say whatever is necessary at the time. For the moment I do not know."

"Well, he ought to be in that bar in about an hour. Just don't call no attention to yourself and don't start no commotion."

Then he rode out.

After about a half an hour I told Wilcey to go on into

town. "Just stay out of the way unless it gets real bad. I ain't worried about Chulo, but he can be pretty serious sometimes, and I don't want him roping the guy and dragging him out here."

"I understand," he said. Then he saddled up and rode off.

I puttered around the camp, not having much to do, trying to work out the details in my mind of just how I wanted the job to go. I tell you, I was feeling some better for having shot straight with my partners. I'll lie when I have to, but I hate to lie to partners. A man gets started on that practice and pretty soon he won't have any partners.

The morning went slow. I just fretted around camp wondering how Chulo was making out. If it didn't go well, if he got in a mess, the whole job could be finished before it got started. I tried to console myself with thinking that Wilcey would be there and he'd see that it all worked out, but I couldn't keep myself from worrying.

Hell, if the truth were to be known I'd sent Chulo in to bring a man back without really knowing what I was going to do with him if the Mexican was able to get him to camp.

Which isn't the smartest kind of thinking. Especially for a man in my line of work.

Finally I decided to have a drink and just wait and see what was going to happen.

The sun kept getting higher and higher in the sky with no sign of anybody. I sat there, leaning against my saddle, drinking rum and staring down at the creek bed and thinking of all the bad things that were probably happening. I just about had Chulo and Wilcey either in jail or shot dead when I happened to glance toward town and saw three horsemen coming. They were too far off to tell who it was so I rolled around, got out my Henry rifle, and lay behind my saddle watching.

In a few minutes I was able to recognize Wilcey and

Chulo. I got up and put my rifle away and stood there, waiting. They come riding on into camp and, sure enough, they had Martin with them.

I asked Wilcey, as they dismounted, "Any trouble?"

"Naw," he said.

I looked at Chulo next. "What'd you tell him?"

He was uncinching his horse and he turned around and give me them white teeth in his dark face. "I tol' him a man wishes to see hem."

"That's all?"

"Oh, I say one lettle theng more."

"What?"

"I tell hem ef he don't come I cut the balls off a horse and make hem eat them." He said it with that big grin on his face.

I looked up at Martin, who was still sitting on his horse. He looked a little pale and a little more nervous, even more than he had in the bar.

"Step down," I said. "You and I are going to have a little conversation." I nodded at Wilcey. "Unsaddle his horse and stake him out. Me and this gentleman might be here a few minutes."

FOUR

————— ∞ —————

Wilcey said, "He babbled pretty good on the way out here. Nerves, I guess."

We were squatted around the campfire, sitting on our saddles and having a drink. Martin did not look comfortable and he had refused our whiskey. I stared at him while Wilcey talked.

"He guesses now he made a mistake. But when he first approached you he was almost certain that you'd been the man that had killed a political rival of his and, if you had been that man, he wanted to thank you and see if he could do any favors for you."

"Is that a fact," I said. We were talking in front of Martin like he wasn't even there, even though I knew he spoke good English.

"Senor," he said, "this is a misunderstanding. Let us forget it and go our separate ways."

I ignored him and asked Wilcey, "You find out much about him?"

Wilcey nodded. "Yeah. He's a pretty heavyweight politician. Apparently well off. He's a lawyer, but he don't practice it much. Fixing to run for governor of the state."

"Oh, yeah?"

"Yeah," Wilcey said. He got that sardonic grin on his face. "And you'll never guess against who."

"Who?"

"Your girlfriend's husband's daddy. The senior Bustamante."

"The hell you say!"

I stared at Martin for a moment. I asked him, "Senor, you mentioned you might have a job for me in my line of work. I reckoned you figured my line of work was killing. Who did you have in mind?"

He got out that handkerchief and commenced mopping his brow. "Oh, no, no, no, senor. You misunderstood. I meant nothing. It was all a mistake."

I looked over at Wilcey and laughed shortly. "Wouldn't that be something. Talk about happenstance."

"I believe it," he said. "In fact I'd almost bet on it."

I laughed again. Then I got out a cigarillo and lit it and walked away. Chulo was sitting on his saddle drinking rum and looking bored. He wasn't interested in the talk. He'd already done his job and the rest was up to me. I gave him a wink as I passed by on my way to stare at the creek and to think this new situation out.

I stood on the bank, smoking, staring down at the little trickle of water. I figured I ought to be able to make some good out of this news. Finally I slung my cigarette into the creek and turned around and went back and sat down on my saddle facing Martin. He was looking plenty nervous. For a moment I wondered what he thought. If some Nigger Mexican had come in and fetched me out to where a bunch of outlaws were waiting, I reckoned I'd been pretty nervous myself. Wasn't any way that all his money or fine clothes or power could do him a bit of good in his present situation. Well, I was kind of counting on his fear.

I said, "Senor Martin, you said you had a job for me. Was this job the assassination of the senior Bustamante, who is your opponent for the office of governor of this Mexican state?"

He mopped his brow, then the back of his neck, and then his upper lip with that handkerchief. He said, "Please, senor. I am very sorry for this misunderstanding. I ask your thousand pardons. If you will please allow me to ride back to my family and friends, the entire incident will be forgotten and nothing more will be said about it. I have made a mistake and I am truly sorry."

I sat there looking at him so prim and proper in his little short-waisted suit and small tie and handmade boots. Oh, he was a success all right, and I wondered how many he'd stabbed and stepped on in getting to be a success. And now the sonofabitch wanted me to help him with some more of his work.

I said, "Senor, I asked you a question. Answer me."

He waved the handkerchief in the air trying to dry it, I guessed, from all the sweat he'd soaked it with. "Please, say no more of this. A mistake."

"No. Who is it you want me to kill?"

He looked mighty upset about those plain words. "Please. Let us not speak of killing. That is not for a man such as myself."

To my right Wilcey laughed. "Boy, he's a prize, ain't he?"

I said to Martin, "I asked you a question, senor. Who is it you want me to kill and what will you pay?"

"I am sorry," he said. "I will not speak of this. Please."

I glanced to my left. "Chulo?"

"*Si?*"

"Cut his ear off."

He got up immediately, *"Si. Como no."* Why not.

He started walking toward our guest digging in his pocket for that big clasp knife of his with the long sharp blade. When he unfolded it the sun caught the shining steel and glinted. I glanced over at Martin. His face had gone white and his eyes had gotten as big and round as saucers. He looked quickly at me. "This is a joke, senor. *Una broma."*

I shook my head. "No. I am a very serious man. Chulo is going to cut your ear off and make you eat it."

"No!" he said. He stood up and tried to walk backwards as Chulo approached, but the saddle was behind his feet and he stumbled over it and fell to the ground. Chulo stood over him, those white teeth large in his black face, the eye patch making him look like the devil come by noon's clear light.

"Wilcey," I said, "get him up on his feet and hold his head so Chulo can cut his ear off."

"Right," Wilcey said. He went over and jerked the senor up, none too gently. The little man was about to faint. His legs had gone weak and rubbery. He was babbling. "No, no, no," he said. "This is not civilized. Surely you do not mean it. Please. Anything."

Wilcey said, "It matter which ear?"

"No. But, Chulo, cut it clean off at the side of his head. Don't make a sloppy job of it."

Our man was about done for. Wilcey had to hold him up because his knees kept buckling. Chulo was standing beside him, stropping that bright, shining blade on his boot toe. "Don't worry, senor," he told Martin. "I fex it good. Real queck."

"No, no, no! Please."

I let Chulo get him by the ear and set the edge of that knife blade against the flesh. Then I asked him, "You want to answer my question, senor?"

He was gasping for breath, almost unable to talk, but he squeezed out a "*Si!* Yes! Please!"

"Sit him down on the saddle," I said. "And give him a drink. He didn't want our whiskey before, but I'll bet he'll take it now."

They got him sat down and Wilcey handed him a tin cup full of rum. Chulo was still standing over him. He acted disappointed. "You mean I don't get to cut his ear off?"

"Not just yet," I said. "Maybe later."

Martin had the cup of rum to his mouth, sucking at it like a baby after a sugar tit. When he was finished draining it he hung his head, panting.

"You ready to answer me?" I asked him.

"He might need some more rum," Wilcey said. It was clear he didn't like our little Mexican friend.

"No," I said. "We'll talk first." I got out another cigarillo and lit it. "Senor, who did you want to hire me to kill?"

He didn't look up so Chulo reached down, got him by the hair, and jerked his head up. "*Es* no good manners," the black Mex said. "You must look at the senor with your eyes when he talk you."

I asked him again. "Who you want to hire me to kill?"

Chulo had his head jerked back and I reckon it was hard for him to talk for his voice come out like a croak. He said, "No."

"Ah, shit!" I said. "Fuck it, Chulo. Cut off both his goddamn ears." I got up as if to walk away and Martin screamed at me, "No, no! I tell you!"

I looked around at him. "Then tell me."

He said, gasping like a fish out of water, "Eduardo Bustamante. The senor opposing me for governor."

I came back and sat down on my saddle. "Turn him loose, Chulo. Wilcey, give him another drink."

He damn near jerked that tin cup out of Wilcey's hand

and threw his head back and drained it at a gulp. When he was through, he sat there panting. I asked him, "Now. You ready to talk a little business?"

"Yes," he said. "Yes. Anything."

"You want me to kill Eduardo Bustamante? Is that right?"

"Yes," he said. He was still panting.

"What will you pay?"

"Anything." He wouldn't look at me. "Whatever you ask."

Chulo was still standing beside him, but Wilcey had gone back and sat on his saddle, looking at the little Mexican politico like you might examine a bug.

I asked him, casually, "How about a thousand dollars? In gold."

He looked up at that and you could see the greedy little bastard inside. A minute before he'd been afraid for his life and his ears, but now we were talking money and I had his attention. He said, "That is a great sum, senor."

"No, it isn't," I said. "With Bustamante out of the way you'll be governor and you can steal a thousand times that much. Maybe more."

"Of course more," Chulo said. He laughed. "We only rob with the *pistole*. We are very *chiquita*. A politico *jefe*, he *es muy grande*."

I said to Martin, "All right? A thousand dollars in gold?"

I had his attention. He blinked at me a few times. Then he looked up at Chulo. Then back at me. "I would in no way be involved? No one would know?"

"That is correct," I said. "However, I will need some information from you. And you will have to make some arrangements."

"Of what nature?"

"We'll discuss that when the question of the money is settled."

He looked up at Chulo again and then over at me. Finally he nodded. "I agree. One thousand dollars in gold."

I said, "No, wait. I have a better thought. If I only kill the senior Bustamante, it may not be complete. After all, the son is an important man. The president of the bank. Married to the daughter of a man who is also influential. I think it would be better to kill both father and son. That way there would be no further trouble from the Bustamante family. Do you not agree?"

He was staring at me, startled. "I do not understand you."

I said, "I will kill them both. But for that I will require fifteen hundred in gold. I don't ask the same price for the son as I do the father, for even a gringo like myself can recognize that they are not of equal value."

Off to my right I saw Wilcey suddenly give me a sharp look. He started to speak, but I held my hand up for him to keep his mouth shut.

I looked steadily at Martin. "Do you not agree?"

He opened his mouth then shut it. Then he got out that goddamn handkerchief again. "I see no need to kill the son."

"Oh, yes," I said. I gave him a little slight grin. "Let us remember that I am the political assassin here. You must be guided by me in these matters."

"I don't know," he said.

I glanced at Chulo. "What do you think, Nigger?"

He drew himself up, enjoying the joke we were playing. "I thenk whatever you thenk, Senor Weelson."

"See?" I said. I held out a hand, palm up. "Even one of your own countrymen agrees. Do you not?"

"Yes," he said, mopping his brow. "Yes, yes. yes."

"Good." I stood up. "Now we have the business part to transact. My friend," I motioned at Chulo, "will accompany you back to town. I want a thousand dollars in gold to seal the bargain. It is just barely the nooning hour and the banks will still be open. He will go in with you and you will give him the thousand dollars and he will bring it back. After that you have nothing to worry about."

That caught him off guard. It was one thing to talk about paying a thousand dollars; it was another to actually have to do it. He opened his mouth to say something and then went to switching his eyes around looking, I reckoned, for a way out of his predicament. He said, "I had not expected payment so soon. And it is a great sum. Let us say five hundred dollars now and the balance when you have completed the work."

I shook my head. "That is not the way I do business. Be very careful that you do not insult me, Senor Martin. I am very skillful in my business, and it is an insult for you to even have the slightest doubt that I cannot kill two Mexicans." I said it grimly, almost sounding angry.

"Oh," he said hastily, "I meant no insult. A thousand pardons. I was unfamiliar with your way of business."

"That's better," I said. "Chulo, saddle Senor Martin's horse for him. After all, he will be the next governor of the state, and it would not do for him to saddle his own horse."

Wilcey had been having trouble the whole time, keeping a straight face, and now he had to turn away to keep from laughing out loud.

When they were saddled and mounted I walked up to where I could take his horse by the bridle. "One other little thing, Senor Martin. We have frightened you and rightfully so for we are three very desperate men. We are all killers, not just myself. Now, perhaps, once you are back in the safety of the town it will occur to you to tell the *policia* or the *Federales* about what we have done to you, and they might kill or capture my friend here." I nodded at Chulo. "And then you might think that you could bring the *policia* back here and they would do the same to me and my other friend. Do not joke yourself. It would be very dangerous. For we will never be found all together at any one time. You might get one of us. You might even get two. But while one was still alive he would kill you, Senor Martin. He would also kill your family. There would be no place that you would be safe. Look carefully into our faces and you will see the truth of what I say."

He glanced at Wilcey, then at Chulo, and lastly came back to me. Then he dropped his eyes. "I understand," he said. Some of the nervous life had gone out of him. He was beaten and he knew it.

"Do not even consider treachery, Senor Martin. Not if you wish to become older. For your safety my friend who is going in with you should be back here in two hours with the gold."

He was still staring down at his saddle horn. "It will be as you say."

"Good." I glanced at Chulo. "Make it pronto, Nigger."

They rode out. We stood there watching until they topped a little rise and disappeared on the other side. Wilcey said, "Will, what the hell are you up to?"

I shook my head and turned away to get a cup of rum and water. "I don't quite know. But I think it'll work."

Wilcey followed me. "Now I know," he said, "that you ain't going to do that greasy little bastard any favors by killing anybody for him. But I can't see where he could be any help to us in robbing that bank."

I sat down on my saddle and sipped at my drink. "We ain't going to rob this bank like any bank you've ever seen robbed before."

"What do you mean?"

I said, "I don't know."

"I mean, how we going to do it then?"

"I don't know yet, Wilcey. Not exactly." I looked over at

him. "Look, I'm not lying to you. I got a bunch of details to work out in my head and when I get it figured exactly I'll tell you. But right now I don't even much want to talk about it. All I got is a hunch that this little greaser is going to be able to help us."

He said, "You—" then stopped.

I looked over at him. "What?"

"Aw, I better not say. It's liable to set off that hair trigger of yours."

"What is it?"

"Well . . . Oh, hell. You ain't really planning on killing them Bustamantes are you?"

I gave him a slow grin. "Never can tell."

"Damnit, Will, don't even joke like that. It ain't funny."

I just shrugged and kept grinning.

"No," he said, "you ain't like that. I know you too well."

But a little while later he said, "Goddamn, you gave that little Mex a rough time. I know you didn't mean it, but you sounded meaner than Chulo looks. Hell, you wouldn't really have taken his ears off, would you?"

I sipped at my drink and didn't say anything.

He said, "Naw, you wouldn't have. You're tough as hell, but you ain't mean. Not like that."

I said, "Whatever you say."

He got up stiffly. "Aw, fuck you. I know when you're playing me. Well, it won't walk." And he went stalking away.

Which made me laugh. For it was normally him that got under *my* skin with that little shit-eating grin of his.

Later he asked me if I didn't think we'd better move the camp. I shook my head. "No. I don't think our greaser friend is foolish enough to cause any trouble. I give him a good enough scare that I trust him not to get any wrong ideas."

"When we going to pull this job?"

"Pretty quick now," I said. "Maybe in a couple of days. Now that I've got Mister Martin to get me the information I need it ought to go pretty fast. I'm going in in the morning and tell him what I want him to find out."

"Is that wise? I mean you going? Why don't you just send Chulo in to bring him out like you done before."

I laughed shortly. "Because I don't think he'd come. For any reason. This time he'd probably think I was going to cut his tongue out just to be sure he didn't talk."

Wilcey said, thoughtfully, "Might not be such a bad idea."

Just about the time I was starting to get worried Chulo came riding back in. "Hallo," he said cheerfully. He got down and unsaddled his horse and turned him out on a picket rope.

"You're damn near late," I said. "I was getting worried. It go all right?"

"Si, que no," he said. He got his saddlebags and came over, pulling out a bottle of cognac. "I find this good brandy. I got four bottles."

"Goddamnit, you Nigger *Meskin!* I didn't send you in to bring back brandy. I sent you in for one thousand dollars in gold."

"Oh, chure," he said. He reached in the other side of his saddlebags and brought out a cloth sack.

I took it and looked inside. It was full of gold pesos. "Is this a thousand dollars?"

He was uncorking a brandy bottle. "The senor say it pretty close. He say he figure it the best he can."

I looked at him. "Why didn't you show me the gold first? Instead of the goddamn brandy. I ought to cut *your* goddamn ears off."

"Why you worry?" he said cheerfully. "It was a small

matter. The senor was very good about it. He only sweat a lettle." Chulo laughed.

"Give me that bottle, goddamnit," I said. I reached over and jerked the brandy out of his hand. "You goddamn heathen," I said. But I was feeling mighty pleased inside. I took a long drink and then passed it along to Wilcey. "Well," I said to him, "you said we wouldn't make no money on this job and we've already made a thousand. How does that strike you?"

He drank and then shook his head at me. "You are the luckiest sonofabitch I've never known. We ought to take that thousand and run like hell."

I laughed. "No, I don't think so, grandmother. We done bought Mister Martin. He belongs to us now. I'm going in in the morning and meet him for coffee and find out what I need to know. We ought to be able to pull this thing . . . What is today, Tuesday?"

"Yeah," Wilcey said. "I think."

"We ought to be able to do it Friday morning. Early."

Wilcey said, "I still don't see how this Martin greaser can help us rob that bank?"

"You will," I said. Then I turned to Chulo. "Now tell me exactly how it went, Nigger. Tell me everything you can remember."

FIVE

I dawdled around camp the next morning, not wanting to start for town much before the sun was about midway in the sky. I knew Martin took his coffee about ten of a morning, and I didn't want to be there too much in advance for I didn't want to spend enough time in town to call attention to myself. I rode out with Wilcey's words in my ears: "Now, Will, you be careful. Because if you don't, if you get in trouble, you're going to get both me and Chulo killed trying to get you out of it."

I rode slowly into town, tied my horse in front of the hotel, and then went on in to the bar. Looking at the sun I'd judged I wouldn't have too long a wait. Not if Senor Martin kept his usual morning coffee time. If he didn't I intended to look him up at my own convenience.

I went into the bar and sat down and ordered a coffee with brandy in it. Then I lit a cigarillo and sat there smoking and sipping at my coffee. I pretty well had the place to myself.

There was only one other customer and he was back in a far corner reading the paper.

Well, I didn't have too long to wait. About the time I was starting on my second coffee and brandy the door opened and Senor Martin, a paper under his arm, came bustling in.

Then he saw me and stopped dead in his tracks, his face pale. I motioned for him to come over. He didn't want to and at first he didn't think he was going to. But I kept motioning and then said, in a loud voice, "Senor Martin, come and have a coffee with me."

That fetched him. He hurried over to the table, glancing around nervously, and sat down in the chair I shoved out with my boot. "Is this wise?" he asked, blotting at his face with the damn handkerchief. "For us to be seen together thusly?"

"Very wise," I said. "For me. Now we have been seen together and if anything happens to me I will immediately involve you. You *sabe*, senor?"

I thought he was going to cry. His face fell and he went to work with that goddamn handkerchief again. I swear, for a Mexican, he sweated more than I'd ever seen. Then he commenced shaking his head, "A sad day," he said, "a sad day for an honorable man when I spoke to you."

"Honorable? Don't make me laugh. Honorable men don't hire assassins."

The waiter came over, just then, bringing Martin his coffee. I said, "You better take some brandy in that."

"No," he said, "no, it is too early in the day for me. It would affect my head."

I waited until the bartender had left and then said, "I got some things I need to know. How many people live in Bustamante the junior's house?"

"The son?"

"Yes."

"I don't understand, senor."

"You ain't supposed to understand. I just want to know how many people live in that goddamn house."

"Two. Eduardo Bustamante and his wife."

"No children?"

"No, senor. It is said that the lady is barren."

Well, I don't know why, but it made me feel a hell of a lot better that she hadn't had any children by that little sonofabitch that had stolen my woman. I don't know why it should have made me feel any better, but it did. I guess it was because children between them would have really made her belong to him.

But that was all a crazy calf kind of thinking. She *was* his woman. Children or not. And what I had to do was find a way to get her out of my mind.

Which was what I was going to do.

I said, "Who else lives there? How many servants?"

"I don't know, senor."

"Find out," I said. "And by this afternoon."

He looked around nervously, scared, I guess, that our conversation might be overheard. But the bartender was at the far end of the bar and the man in the corner was still reading his paper.

"This is important?"

"Yeah," I said. "And how close does the Bustamante senior live to his son's house?"

"Very *proxima*. Very close. I do not understand."

"You're not supposed to understand. Now. Can you gain an entrance to either house?"

He looked surprised. "But of course. I am friends of both the families."

Well, that disgusted me. Here he was, thinking he'd paid me to shoot both of them, and he was still describing himself as a friend of the family. I said, "I thought you wanted them dead?"

Now he looked puzzled. "But that is politics, senor. Of course we are friendly. That is the civilized way. Sometimes we drink coffee in this very bar together."

I just shook my head. Sometimes, as bad as I felt about being a robber and a killer, I sometimes wondered if I wasn't more honest than a sonofabitch like this little killer in his neat suit and his carefully tied tie. Drinking his coffee with his paper under his arm and plotting the murder of a friend.

"All right," I said. I called the bartender for my score. After I'd paid and the bartender had left, I got up. I said to Martin, "This afternoon at about four o'clock you are to ride out toward where we are camped and bring me the information I want about Bustamante the junior's house. Don't fail to be there."

"Senor, I'm not sure."

I just gave him a look. "You be there, Martin, or you got plenty of trouble." Then I turned and walked out and got on my horse.

I knew where I was going, but I didn't like to think I was. So I just tried not to think. I let my horse slow walk down the street and then to the left and keep walking until we were at the Bustamante's house. It hurt me to be out there in the street, looking at the house of another man, knowing she was in there as his wife.

I sat there a long time, just smoking and thinking. I don't know what I'd of done if she'd suddenly have walked out the front door. But, hell, I didn't even know if I'd recognize her. She might have gone to fat and been as ugly as homemade sin by now.

But I didn't believe it for a moment.

Then I got to wondering if she'd recognize me. Well,

there was no reason she should, not as long as it had been.

But I was damn well going to remind her of who I was when the time came.

I turned my horse and started back into town, my mood not particularly good. I needed a woman. I could feel it inside myself, so I walked my horse up a back street, looking for the little cantina that Chulo had frequented with such good effect. I didn't have much trouble finding it. It had come the siesta hour and the street was quiet, but the cantina was open. There were a couple of Mexicans sleeping on the sidewalk, leaned back up against the building, their sombreros shading their eyes. I clumped by them, my spurs *clinging* on the hard-packed dirt, pushed open the door of the cantina, and went on in. It was dark and cool inside, and I took a moment to let my eyes adjust. The room looked empty except for a bartender leaning over his bar swatting lazily at flies with a wet towel. I went on up and leaned against the bar and ordered brandy. He shrugged, *"Yo no tengo,"* he said.

"Then give me the good tequila. The best you have."

He brought me a bottle and a glass, and I poured out and knocked the burning liquid down my throat. He'd set a half a lime down beside the bottle, and I sucked on that to cut the oily taste out of my mouth. Then I put a little salt on the back of my hand and picked at that. In a moment I felt better. Tequila ain't bad if that's all you can get.

Then I looked around and realized that I wasn't alone in the bar. My eyes had adjusted and I could see a Mexican at a back table slumped down resting his head on his arms. There was a guitar on the tabletop, and I figured he was a musician of some kind. I turned around to the bartender and asked him where the girls were. He shrugged and said they were all asleep, that they were taking the siesta.

"Wake them up," I said in Spanish.

He shrugged again. "That is not possible, senor. Now is the time for rest. They work very hard *a las noches.*"

I said, "I ain't interested in what they did last night. I'm only interested in right now. So you go damn quick and wake them up. You *sabe?*"

He looked a little alarmed at my tone, sort of half straightening up out of the fat-bellied slough he was in. "Senor," he said, "it would be trouble for me if I were to do such a thing."

I pulled out my big .44-40 revolver and laid it on the bar. Then I said, "You're going to get in a hell of a lot more trouble with me if you don't. You *sabe* me?"

His eyes got as big around as the bottom of a tequila bottle. He said, "Aiee, senor. *Si, quehe no!* Yes, of course."

"Then go and do it," I said.

He went hurrying off in a kind of waddling trot, and I took my bottle and glass and sat down at a table to wait.

I knew what I was doing wasn't very smart. You don't want to go causing a commotion when you're about to rob a bank. But my mood was bad and the girl Linda was still in my heart, and I just frankly didn't give a damn if school kept or not.

The guitar player was still slumped over his table and I turned around and yelled at him. "Hey! Hey! *Marachi!*"

A *marachi* being a strolling musician.

He didn't budge so I yelled at him again. He still lay there, a sombrero on the back of his head, his face cradled in his arms. "Goddamnit!" I said. "Wake up! I want some music?"

He still didn't raise his head so I took a shot glass that had been sitting on the table and flung it at him. It hit him on the shoulder and he raised his head, unfolding his arms as he did. But it wasn't a Mexican musician's face I was looking at; it was the business end of a very big *pistola*. And the face behind it wasn't Mexican at all.

He said, "What the hell you want?"

"Oh, shit!" I said.

It was Sam Jackson, a half-breed Cherokee and Irishman that I'd been knowing for any number of years. Of course there wasn't a sign of Indian in him from his mother's side; he was all Irish-looking and about as red-headed and pink-faced as a baby's bottom. But he could pass for a Mexican, for there are a lot of red-faced Mexicans, and besides, the sonofabitch spoke fluent Spanish.

"Shit," I said again, "it ain't no *marachi*. It ain't nobody but Sam Jackson. Put that goddamn *pistola* down, before I take it away from you."

He kind of straightened up and give me a closer look. "Wilson? Is that Will Young?"

"Hell, yes, you dumb sonofabitch. Come over here and tell me why you ain't in jail."

"Well, I be go to hell," he said. He got up, pushing his sombrero back and come over, sticking that big *pistola* down in his waistband as he walked. We shook and he sat down and grinned at me. Sam always was a funny little bastard. I'd never rode with him or done no business with him, but I knew him to be a good man from what I'd heard from others. Only bad new I'd ever heard on him was that he liked to get a little comical at the wrong times. But, hell, ours is a serious business enough as it is, and it never hurts a man to laugh once in a while.

He sat down and I poured us out a drink in the glasses that was scattered on top of the table, and we said luck and then knocked them straight back as befits the toast. I asked him what he was doing in Sabinas Hidalgo.

He kind of shrugged. "Oh, sort of hiding out. I done a little business down around Brownsville and the country got a little warm for me, so I taken it south to parts that was friendlier."

I nudged the guitar that he'd brought over to my table. "And what the hell's that for?"

"I can play the damn thing," he said. "Didn't you know that?" He picked it up and strummed a few respectable chords. "Learned at first from my daddy. That shanty Irish bastard. Then learned better from a wore out dance hall queen I was living with when I was about sixteen."

I laughed. Hell, you had to laugh around Sam. Though, make no mistake, he was tough enough when he had to be.

He asked me what I was doing so far south in Mexico. I just shrugged and told him about the same as he'd told me. I didn't much want him to know we had business in town. Not right then, anyway.

His real Indian name was Owl of the Night Jackson. I don't know where he picked up the Sam. It had kind of surprised me running into him, but then I'm a man as will take luck anywhere he finds it, and I was beginning to think he was luck. For the last couple of days the plan I'd been working on in my mind needed a fourth man; not only a fourth man, but a Mexican, and not no Mexican that looked like Martin, neither. Of course we had Chulo, but I needed me a Mexican that looked like a town Mexican and old Sam sure enough looked that in his sombrero and serape and them peon pants they wear.

But about then the girls come in. There was three of them and they come in looking frowsy and irritated about being waked up and just generally sullen. Two of them wasn't much, as you'd expect, but one didn't look so bad. They sat down and the bartender immediately brought them over some kind of a drink. Then he looked at me and shrugged as if to say, "I have done my best."

When Sam Owl saw the girls he laughed. "So," he said.

"So, this is what Wilson Young is doing in such a cantina. Well, why not!"

"Go to hell, Sam," I said.

He laughed again. *"Como no.* You want some help, *amigo?"*

I said, "I don't need no help from such as you."

"No? Then you watch."

And, damned if he didn't go over to them girls and start strumming on that damned guitar of his. He sang some Spanish words in their ears, going from one to the other. And you could see them perking up.

I said, "What the hell."

And he turned around and give me that damn Irish grin of his. "You like?" he said.

"Go to hell," I said.

Well, he went on strumming that goddamn guitar and singing to them *putas,* and I be damned if they didn't start glowing. Then they commenced looking over at me. I couldn't hear what he was whispering low to them in Spanish, but it seemed to be having a pretty good effect.

I said, "You seem to be pretty well acquainted around here. At least for a half-breed."

"Oh, yes," he said. "For a handsome man with a guitar it doesn't take long."

"Shit!" I said. "Listen, leave them girls alone and come over here and talk to me about some business. But tell them not to go away. I'll get to them directly."

I poured us out another drink of tequila and considered about Sam. He seemed just about perfect for what I had in mind. I glanced over at him. "You in the mood to do a little business?"

He got out a cigarillo and lit it. "Always ready to do some business with you, Will. Little surprised at the honor. I'm kind of small potatoes alongside of you. What you got in mind?"

"Well," I said, "I don't much want to talk about it right now. How long you say you been in town?"

"Oh, 'bout a month I'd reckon."

"I guess you know it pretty well by now, you and your guitar."

"You can laugh all you want about that guitar, but ain't nobody takes me for a robber, neither. Yeah, I know most of the folks here. Or at least I know who they are."

"This ain't your hidey-hole is it?"

"You mean, would I not want to do business here?" He shook his head. "Naw. It's jest a place I stopped. Was planning on pulling out anyway. I reckon you must be talking doing some big business, Will. You know my reputation. I ain't never been much besides a small-time cattle thief."

"You'll be all right," I said. "What I got in mind ought to be up your alley. Now tell you what. Me and my two partners got a camp out north of here on that little creek. You ride out there about dusk and I'll tell you what I got in mind. Might be a good idea we don't get seen together until we pull this."

He got up, taking his guitar. "Them two partners of your'n. Do I know 'em?"

"Might know one. I doubt you know Wilcey."

He shook his head.

"The other one is the Mexican Chulo. The one they call Nigger."

He laughed shortly. "You mean the one they call the mean sonofabitch. Yeah, I know him. Not real good. More by reputation."

"That's the one," I said. "But you go ahead and get on out

of here and then hunt us up this evening about dusk. We'll
build up the fire to give you a signal."

"I'll be there." He started off then glanced at the girls and
then back at me. "Give 'em a good fight, Will," he said. He
laughed.

"Get out of here."

When he was gone I motioned for the best looking of the
three girls to come over to my table. She slouched over and
sat down, not looking too interested. Well, to tell you the
truth, I wasn't that interested myself. I was more angry than
I was filled with lust; angry at myself for letting that girl
Linda put me in the shape I'd gotten in, angry that I was
maybe about to pull one of the dumbest jobs I ever had,
angry that she was over there in that house with her little
husband.

I looked at the girl, trying to think of something to say.
She was about on an average with every Mexican whore I'd
ever taken to bed. She wasn't bad, but she wasn't that pretty
neither. She was a little plump and looked to have a little
Indian blood in her, judging from the flatness of her face.
Her breasts were large, but they just kind of sagged down
against the material of her bodice.

But, what the hell, who was I to be choosy at that point?

I didn't much want to talk to her. All I wanted to do was
relieve myself in a woman, any woman, and hope that it
would cut through a little of the pain I was feeling inside. So
I just asked her where her room was and, when she nodded
toward a little hall that ran off one side of the main room, I
got up and pulled her to her feet and set off. "Com'on,
woman," I said to her, "we're going to war."

Before the day was out I ended up taking all three of them
back to the room. I couldn't tell if it helped or not. I felt tired
and drained, but I couldn't feel any change in either my
spirit or my mood.

Of course they had got glad for the unexpected afternoon trade and what with a few drinks and the fact that I was paying better than they'd of expected, had quit being sulled up and was downright friendly. But the afternoon had wore away, and it had come time for me to meet Martin out on the edge of town. I made my adios, got a couple of bottles of brandy from the barkeep, paid my score, and left. It was a little later than I'd expected, so I urged my horse into a slow lope and rode about a half mile out of town, looking for Martin. There was no sign of him, so I pulled up in the shade of a tall mesquite tree, lit a cigarillo, and waited for him to show up.

He was a long time in coming—so long, in fact, that I was beginning to think I'd been late myself and missed him. Finally, however, I seen a horseman appear out of the buildings of the town and come in my direction. He come slowly, hesitantly, but it wasn't long before I was able to recognize Martin.

He rode like a man who didn't much like where he was going, and it took him what seemed forever to get to my side. When he finally did pull his horse up, I was sitting there with one leg hooked around the saddle horn drinking brandy out of the bottle.

He looked mighty nervous, like he was afraid he was going to get his ears cut off again. He said, "As you can see I am here."

I said, "You taken your own sweet time getting here."

"There was business and it was not so easy to get what you asked for and do it very carefully."

"Well? Then tell me."

He looked around nervously again, as if he half expected somebody to be spying on us out there in the middle of the bald ass prairie. "Take it easy, Martin," I told him. "Only worry you got is if you didn't find out what I told you to."

"I have it," he said. But he had to get out that damn handkerchief and give his face a mopping before he could tell me. "There are only the three servants," he said. "One is the boy who takes care of the carriage and the horses. He lives in the stable. Then there are a man and a woman for the house and for the care of the senora."

"Is that all?" It didn't sound like enough to me. "For that big house?"

"Yes. It is because there is only the senor and the senora. And they do not receive many visitors. Yes. That is all. *El todas*."

I looked at him closely, but I didn't figure him to be lying, not at this stage, not in as deep as he was. But I kept looking at him, making him jittery. I had a hard piece of orders I was fixing to give him, and I wanted him good and softened up. I said, "All right, for your sake I hope what you say is correct." He started to protest that he'd done his best to do as I'd asked, but I cut him off. "Never mind that," I said. "Now, in the morning, I want you to be at Bustamante the junior's front door at exactly seven o'clock of the morning."

It kind of took him off balance. "Be at— But what for?"

"Never mind that," I said. "You just be there. I will be with you. I will tell you in the morning what you are to do and say."

He commenced making sounds like he wasn't going to do it. "But, senor, I cannot be mixed up in this! If I'm seen there with you there will be much trouble for me. Oh, no, no, no!"

I told him to shut up. "Now listen, Martin, you're going to do as you're told or else you ain't going to have to worry about trouble from nobody because I'll give you enough to last you the rest of your life. Now you just take it easy until I tell you what it's all about."

Well, that settled him down some. I pitched him the bottle

of brandy, and he had a big pull and then wiped his mouth with the handkerchief. "Now," I said, "this ain't in no way going to get you connected with me. As a matter of fact it's going to make you look like one of the victims yourself. You *sabe?* If anything it will make you look blameless. As if you'd had no part in the affair. I have this very carefully planned and, believe me, if you do the little thing I want you to do, you will come out very well indeed."

Well, he didn't look completely satisfied, but he didn't look so nervous either. He said, "I am to do just one little thing and then my part in the affair is finished?"

"For sure. And it will be a very little thing. No more than knocking on the door and telling the servant that you want to speak to Bustamante the junior."

"That is all?"

"That's all. And in no way will you be connected with me. But you must be there at seven o'clock of the morning for sure. Can you manage that?"

He stalled a minute, looking at it from all sides, but then he finally shrugged. "But of course. Yes, I believe I can."

I figured I might as well make a little more profit on the deal so I said, just as I turned my horse away, "And be sure and have the rest of the money with you. Once we've done the job we won't have time to stop and collect. You *sabe?*"

"Yes," he said. "Yes, of course."

Last look I took at him as I rode away he was busy mopping his face with that handkerchief. Man must have had to buy them by the gross.

I rode back to the camp in a kind of thoughtful mood. I'd make my plans and, near as I could figure, we were all ready to go. Only thing I didn't know was would it work or not. And, since, I didn't know if anybody had ever tried to rob a bank in the way I was figuring on doing, I didn't have much to go on.

But, hell, the dice were cast. All I could do was wait and see what numbers come up.

My partners were eating a pot of beans they'd bought off a woman in town. I rode in, unsaddled, picketed my horse, and then come up to the fire. Wilcey said, "Where the hell you been all day?"

"Fucking whores," I said. Chulo laughed.

I got a plate of beans and a handful of tortillas and sat down and commenced eating. Chulo handed me over a cup of coffee.

"Well?" Wilcey said, after a minute.

"Let me eat these beans," I said. "I'm hungry as hell."

Chulo laughed again. "Fucking makes a man *muy hambre*."

I ate in silence until I was through then set my plate aside, leaned back against my saddle, and sighed. "I didn't know how hungry I was," I said. I lit a cigarillo and sat there smoking and sipping my coffee.

Wilcey said, "You get anything figured out?"

"Got it all figured out," I said.

"Yeah? What are we going to do?"

"We're going to rob a bank."

"Shit, I already knew that. When?"

I paused. "In the morning."

SIX

It was a good long minute before anybody spoke and then Wilcey said, "What? What did you say?"

"You heard me. We're robbing the bank in the morning."

"Shit!" he said. He got up and poured himself another cup of coffee, then found a bottle of brandy and laced it up pretty good with that. Dusk was starting to come in and he looked dark against the sky as the sun sank on down into the horizon. He sat back down. He looked over at me. "You ain't serious? You don't mean that."

I nodded with my face down in my cup of coffee. "Yeah. I mean it."

"Well, just tell me how the hell we can do that? You ain't looked this thing over enough. Was you in that bank today?"

I shook my head. "No. Ain't been near it, but that one time."

"Then what the hell makes you think we're ready to rob that sucker? I never seen you so careless about a job in all the time I've knowed you." He appealed to Chulo. "You think we're ready to rob this bank, Nigger?"

He didn't get much help from Chulo. The black Mexican just laughed. "*Yo no se.*" I don't know. "I am joust a dumb Meskin. Whatever Weelson say. I always make money with Weelson."

"Take it easy, Wilcey," I finally said. "I got it all figured out. Got it planned to the last inch."

"Well, would you mind letting us in on this plan? Or you going to keep it to yourself and let us guess?"

"Wilcey," I said, "I swear, you're getting to be more the old woman every day." Still, I hesitated to lay it all out, at least all at once. I knew what Wilcey would have to say and what he'd accuse me of. But, hell, they had to know sooner or later. I was just fixing to start telling them when there came a holler from out of the dark.

"Halloo the fire! Halloo the camp!"

Wilcey and Chulo immediately got up, reaching for their guns. Wilcey said, "Now who the hell can that be?"

"Most likely our new partner," I said.

Wilcey looked over at me. "New partner? When did this happen?"

"This afternoon," I said. "Run into him in the whore-house. I believe he's just what we need for the way I got this thing set up." I turned into the darkness and yelled, "Is that you, Sam?"

The answer came back, about a hundred yards off. "Oh, yeah!"

"Then ride on in."

"Who is it?" Wilcey asked me.

I nodded over at Chulo. "The Nigger knows him. Sam Jackson? Sam Owl? Half-breed cattle thief."

In the light of the fire I could see Chulo nodding. "*Si.* He's a good hombre."

Wilcey said, "I swear to God, Wilson, you are a hard man to keep up with. Are you sure we can trust this fellow?"

"Now that's a dumb question, Wilcey. You reckon I'd of taken him on if I didn't think so? Hell, have a drink, the moonlight is addling your brain."

"I was just asking."

As quickly as I could I told them about Sam, saying, "I ain't never been on no jobs with him, but the word is he's a good man, especially in a fight." I seen Wilcey give me a quick glance so I said, "Not that I'm expecting a fight. Way I got it planned out I got a very little job for Sam Owl to do, but he looks to be the right one to do it."

Just then the half-breed come riding in and Chulo got up to help him unsaddle and picket his horse. When they come up to the fire, I introduced him to Wilcey and then we poured out some brandy in tin cups and knocked them back for luck.

Sam looked over at Chulo. "*Caramba,* black *Meskin,* you are still as mean-looking as ever. Maybe more so."

We made some more small talk and then I asked Sam Owl if he'd left anything back in town. He looked across at me. "What you mean?"

"Oh, traps, gear."

He give a short laugh. "Ever'thing I own is in them saddlebags. I travel plenty light."

"That's good," I said, "because if you want to throw in with us on this job, you ain't going to have time to go back in and fetch nothing."

"What's the job?"

"We're going to rob the bank. In the morning."

"Just like that?"

"Just like that," I said.

We were sitting on all four sides of the fire, leaned back against our saddles. There was a little wind and you could hear it through the boughs of the willows that lined the creek. I lit a cigarillo and began to lay it out for them, explaining everything except the part that concerned me and the girl, the girl Linda. When I was finished Sam Owl whistled slowly and said, "Hombre, that's slick. I'd heered you could plan a job of robbery, but I ain't never knowed no man could come up with such a plan as that. Hell, count me in for sure."

Wilcey said, "Will, ain't nobody ever tried to rob a bank that way. What makes you think it'll work?"

I shot him a look. "What makes you think it won't?"

He rubbed his jaw, looking worried. But, then, he always looked worried. Seemed to me he'd aged considerable in the few years we'd been riding the outlaw trail together. Sometimes I wondered if Wilcey should have ever turned his hand to such a line of work.

I said, "So that's about it. I figure we'll get somewhere around twenty thousand dollars. Ought to make a good payday and ought not to be a shot fired."

Chulo said, "I thenk we fool one Mexican bank." He laughed, his white teeth flashing in the reflection from the fire.

We talked about it a few minutes more and then I got up to go check on my horse. I heard Wilcey coming behind me, but I just went ahead and checked to make sure my horse was securely picketed and wouldn't wander off during the night. I stood there a moment, looking up at the stars, and sort of patting my horse on the head. Wilcey came up, the glow of his cigarillo marking his coming. It had got pretty dark, though there was no overcast. I marked that fact, that there'd be little moon for the next couple of nights, just in case we had to do any night fleeing.

Wilcey come up and stood a moment beside me before he

spoke. Then he said, "That's the damnedest plan I ever heard of, Will. What caused you to think it up?"

"Damned if I know," I said. "Just seemed like the thing to do at the time."

He stood beside me, drawing on his cigarillo, staring out into the night. "It was on account of that girl, wasn't it? That Linda."

I only hesitated for a second. Then I said, "Yeah."

"That's what I thought."

"It was the only way I could figure to do the two things at the same time—see her and rob the bank."

Around us the several horses made rustling sounds as they grazed through the tall grass. One snorted through his nose, the noise making a large sound in the still night.

Wilcey said, "Well, I hope this finally cures you of her. God knows I'm tired of watching you every time you think of her."

"You can see that?"

"Hell, a blind man can see it. How long's this been going on—six, eight years?"

"Something like that," I said lowly.

"Well, I won't say anything about you being a damn fool. I ain't ever going to talk about any other man being a damn fool over a woman. Lord knows I ain't got the right."

"Then it's okay with you? About what I'm going to do? About the way I got the robbery planned?"

He laughed shortly. "Hell, it has to be. Like Chulo says, 'We do et as the way Mester Weelson say.'" Then he turned to face me. "I don't know how this will go, but I don't figure it's your style to get your partners in a storm over your personal business."

"No," I said.

His face was becoming more distinct in the dark, and I could see him looking at me curiously. "By the way, what are you going to do with her once you have your hands on her?"

I shook my head. "I don't know."

"You ain't going to do anything dishonorable, are you?"

Now I laughed. "That's goddamn funny coming from a killer and a robber."

"You know what I mean."

"Yeah," I said. I flipped away my cigarillo. "Let's go turn in. We going to be up early."

We walked back to the fire and I said, "We better mount a watch tonight. I'm not worried, but it can't hurt. Sam, you take the first one. Then Chulo then Wilcey then me. Make them about two hours each. Somebody bank that fire and let's turn in."

I took a cup of brandy with me when I crawled into my bedroll and then lay there, sipping at it, while I stared up at the sky and wondered if I knew what I was doing. I was tired for some reason and it wasn't long, after I'd slugged down the last swallow of brandy, that I turned over and went straight to sleep.

I awoke sometime early in the morning with Wilcey shaking me by the shoulder. "Will," he said, "Will, your watch."

I rolled over and sat up. It had turned off chilly and the blankets I'd been wrapped in had felt good. There was no moon, but most of the stars were gone and I judged it to be about four o'clock of the morning. I pulled on my boots and sat around sideways. Wilcey had gone over to squat by the fire. He was poking up the coals around the coffeepot. "Makin' some coffee," he said.

"Yeah," I said. "Let me get the cow shit out of my mouth." I stumbled down to the creek and knelt on the bank and washed my mouth out. I shivered just a little in the morning chill. Then I went back up and squatted down by the fire while Wilcey poured us up a couple of cups. "You better get some shut-eye," I said. "Ain't long until dawn."

"Ah," he said, "I'll sit up a little longer. Feels like I've had enough sleep."

Across the fire, now starting to blaze up again, Chulo and Sam Owl were rolled in their blankets. I squatted there, sipping at the steaming coffee. In just a few hours we'd be going on another job, but, for some reason, I didn't feel that tightness in my throat and chest I nearly always felt. There may be them as can spit before a job, but I never been one. Usually my mouth is so dry I have trouble smoking a cigarillo, but, and I couldn't figure it, here we were just some three hours from the job and I wasn't particularly feeling anything.

But Wilcey seemed nervous enough for both of us. I looked over at him, the firelight gleaming off his lean face. "What's the matter, Jesse James," I said, laughing, "rather be home on the farm?"

"You laugh all you want to, but we're about to try and rob a bank in a way ain't never been tried before. I been doing a considerable amount of thinking since I been sitting up. Hell of a lot of things can go wrong."

"Hell, Wilcey," I said, "they's always something can go wrong on a bank robbery. Plenty of things. No matter how you do it. You ought to know by now ain't no sure things in our profession."

"Still—" he said.

"Whyn't you hit your bedroll? We still got a good hour before we have to start getting ready. You'll need the rest later. Take you a pull of that brandy and turn in."

"Well," he said, "I guess." He got up and went over and rolled up in his blankets, leaving me to stare at the fire and drink coffee. My mind kind of drifted back over the years, thinking of all the campfires I'd sat around, all the places I'd been. And now here I was knowing that I'd be seeing her again for the first time in all those years. That I wouldn't be seeing her at her bidding or by her choice really didn't make that much difference. All I could think about was that I'd be seeing her again. She was so much on my mind that I had to keep reminding myself we was also going to rob a bank.

Well, Wilcey had been right. There were a lot of things could go wrong on this job. I had it figured as best I could, but there were an awful lot of people involved, and you get that many all strung around in different places and goddamn near anything could happen.

But the die was cast and I was determined to play out the hand.

I sat there until the first light of the false dawn began to stir in the sky, then I got up and went and roused my partners. "Time to get it," I said. "Everybody up."

Chulo and Sam came up yawning and stretching, but Wilcey rolled right out. I doubted if he'd gone back to sleep.

In a few minutes they were all gathered around the fire drinking coffee and eating cold beef and tortillas. "Don't dawdle," I said. "We got time, but not all that much. And in case I forget it, everybody take plenty of cartridges in their pockets."

Sam said, "Thought you wasn't expecting no shooting."

"I'm expecting everything," I said.

In a little we were getting saddled up. The sun wasn't quite up yet, but the dawn was coming and objects like trees and rocks and hills began to emerge out of the darkness. We used soft cotton ropes for our picket lines for our horses, and I told Chulo to gather them up and put them in his saddlebag.

Wilcey said, "What's that for, Will?"

"Tell you later," I said. "Sam, you get all the canteens and fill them up. If we have to run I don't think we'll have time to stop for water."

I saddled my horse, tied on my bedroll, and then checked my pistol and rifle while I waited on the others. One by one they mounted up and stood waiting. I roused myself just as the sun edged over the horizon and swung into the saddle.

"Let's go to town," I said, "and rob a bank."

We set off at a good steady trot. There was time, but not too much. I didn't want to be late, but I also didn't want to be so early that we'd be hanging around town long enough to call attention to ourselves.

When the sun was up good and we were still about a half mile from town, I pulled us up and dismounted. "Ever'body get down," I said. "I want to go over all this one more time."

I searched around until I found a stick, then I smoothed off a place on the sandy prairie and squatted down to draw out a map of the Bustamante's house.

"This is the main house," I said. I drew a square in the sand, then drew a bigger one around it. "And this is the fence around it. It's more for looks than anything else. I don't even think these here gates lock. But even if they do, you oughtn't to have any trouble getting through them." I tapped the front of the house with my stick. "Now here's where I'm coming in. With Martin. Wilcey, you and Chulo and Sam will come around here to the back. You and Sam wait outside the gate while Chulo goes in." I drew a little square behind the bigger square that was the house. "Now here's the stable. Like I told you, Martin says the boy who takes care of the carriages and the horses sleeps in there. More than likely he'll be either in the stable or stirring around outside somewhere. Now, Chulo, you go in quietly and take him in. Don't kill him unless you have to, and if you do have to, for God's sake don't fire a gun. Knife him or something."

I looked up at the big Mexican and he nodded.

"Then, after you have the boy in hand, go over and knock on the gate and then"—I looked up—"Wilcey, you and Sam come in. You know you're bringing all the horses in. Put them in the stable and be goddamn sure you shut that fence gate. Somebody come along and see something and we're a bunch of blowed-up suckers. Of course," and I motioned with the stick out behind the back gate, "this is mostly open field out here, so I don't really reckon anybody's going to be wandering around out there."

I pointed at the back of the house. "Now I imagine the back door is about here. I've never seen it, but it's got to be somewhere around in here. Y'all wait until I open that door before you come in. And Chulo, don't forget the rope." I stood up. "That ought to about do it until we get in the house. After that I ain't so sure."

As we mounted up Wilcey asked me if I was sure Martin would show up as planned. I shrugged. "I damn well hope so. And my guess is that he will. But even if he don't, I might still be able to get in that front door on my own. But we'll cross that bridge when we come to it."

We set off toward town at a good canter. I judged it to be about ten or fifteen minutes before seven.

When we hit the outskirts I led us around to the left, just hanging along behind the last line of buildings. When I figured we were about a hundred yards from Bustamante's house, I pulled us up and then walked the horses forward until we could just see it. "Now that's it," I said. I dismounted and handed my reins to Wilcey. "Give me around five minutes. No more. Wilcey, if you and Sam hear any trouble from the inside get right on in, don't wait for Chulo to let you in." I looked up at the Mexican sitting on his horse. "Now, Chulo, remember— You got to gather up anybody that comes out that back door. I'll have them stopped from the front, but you got to stop them at the back. If I'm lucky I'll be able to get everybody under my gun at the same time, but it might not work out that way, so be ready for anything. All right, good luck and I'll see y'all inside the house."

I turned and went walking toward Bustamante's house. As I went I loosened my revolver in its holster. Now, finally, I was starting to feel a little on edge. I couldn't see the front of the house yet, so I didn't know if Martin was there or not. Then I turned the corner and he was standing there, just in front of the fence gate. Damned if he wasn't wiping his forehead with his handkerchief, and as cool as it was, I knew it wasn't the weather making him sweat. He had a bag in his hand, a bag that looked to contain gold coins. When he saw me he gave a little start and put his hand to his heart. Oh, he was scared and make no mistake.

"Hello, Martin," I said, as I came up to him. "Nice morning."

"Senor," he said. "Senor, I—"

"Let's go," I said. I reached over and opened the fence gate. The fence was a high one, better than six feet, and the door was solid wood, but it wasn't locked. I motioned for Martin to go ahead.

He didn't move, just stood there clutching that sack of gold. "Senor," he said again, "Senor, I—I—I—"

"Get in there, Martin!" I said. "I'm in a hurry. Now, move!"

He worked his mouth and finally come out with, "I can't! I can't be mixed up in this. Instead of five hundred dollars, I have brought you one thousand dollars and I ask you to take it and forget that I ever spoke with you. It was my mistake and I will pay you for your troubles."

I took him firmly by the shoulder and shoved him through the gate and shut it behind me. The house was one of the big, two-story haciendas made out of stucco or some such with red tile on the roof and all them arched doorways and windows. There was a big wide porch running around on all three sides that I could see. I took Martin by the arm and pushed him forward. "Too late to back out now," I said. "You get up there and knock on that door. If you're scared of that door, you ain't got no idea how scared you're fixing to get of me."

He went, being pushed by my hand almost more than by his own legs carrying him. When we were at the door I told him, "Now, when the servant answers, you tell him you have an urgent message for Senor Bustamante and to go and fetch his master as fast as possible. Will the servant know your name?"

"Perhaps," he said. He was almost pale and he was shaking and sweating pretty badly.

"Now knock," I said. "Go ahead, knock, damnit!"

He did, reluctantly, and so lightly that I give it a couple of whams myself.

I told him, "Now when Bustamante comes down, you tell him I have an urgent message for him and that you have only guided me to his house. After that you're out of it. You understand, that's all you have to do."

Well, a little relief come over his face as he got to thinking it wasn't going to be as bad as he'd thought.

About then the door swung open and a squat little woman stood there. She had a spoon in her hand like she was cooking and she looked at Martin and then at me. "*Si*, senor?"

In Spanish Martin told her it was urgent that we see the Senor Bustamante. She bowed a little and held the door wider and we walked in. With her following we walked down a little hall and then into a big kind of a sitting room with straight-backed furniture sitting all around. The windows were all open to let in the morning breeze so it was pretty light. There was a stair at the back of the room that led, I guessed, to some sleeping quarters upstairs. There were a few other doors and hallways leading off, but I couldn't cover all those. All I could do was stop up the front and hope that Chulo and the rest could catch up anything that might get out the back. The woman said, *"Momentito,"* and then went off up the stairs.

I glanced at Martin. He was looking nervous again.

Then we got lucky. The other servant, the man came through a door from the kitchen, I reckoned, carrying a tray with coffee on it. He stopped, a little surprised at seeing us. I motioned him to come forward and he brought the coffee and set it on a little table by a big, straight-backed chair. I figured that was where Junior took his coffee every morning. He started to leave the room, but I said, *"Alto,"* stop. In Spanish I said, "You are to remain here. The master is coming."

Well, he looked a little confused, but he stopped and just stood there. He was, like his wife, just an ordinary-looking Mexican house servant. About middle-aged. We wouldn't have any trouble with them.

Then Bustamante came down the stairs buttoning his vest. Even in the morning he looked like the dandy, with his little mustache and his black hair slicked back. The old woman had stayed upstairs, to tend to Linda I guessed. If, indeed, she was up there.

Bustamante advanced across the living room and nodded coolly to Martin. "Senor, good morning." Then he looked at me.

Martin, his voice kind of quavering, said, "Senor Bustamante, a thousand pardons for bothering you so early of the morning, but this *caballero* has an urgent message for you."

I said to Bustamante, as politely as I could make it sound, "Is your wife here, senor?"

He sort of stiffened as if to say it wasn't any of my goddamn business whether she was or wasn't.

"I have a message for her," I said.

"She is in her bedchamber," he said. "Sleeping."

"The message is important."

"You can give it to me. I will relay it to her."

"It concerns her uncle in Villa Union."

"Ah," he said, "Don Fernando." Some of the suspicion left his face.

"Exactly." I was stalling for a little time, trying to be sure and give Chulo enough to get the boy gathered up and let Wilcey and Sam in. I said, "I'm not certain I should speak of it to anyone but her. Will she be asleep much later?"

"I cannot say," he said. "But I am her husband. Deliver the message to me and I'll go upstairs and wake her if the news is of that importance."

"Well, perhaps," I said. I looked around. The old man was still standing there, wondering, possibly, what the hell he was supposed to be doing. I said, "But in private." I pointed at a door. "Is that the kitchen?"

He shook his head. "No, that is the kitchen." He pointed to a door a little further back. "But why—"

I said, "If you'll just step back there with me I'll give you the message."

He looked confused at my request, but then he shrugged. "If it is necessary."

"Please," I said. I glanced at Martin. "I will be but a very few seconds, senor. Wait." I put a little menace in the word.

Still looking uncertain, Bustamante led me through a big door into the kitchen. It was a long room with a cast-iron stove and a fireplace. As we went through the door I drew my pistol, cocking it as I did. He heard the *clitch clatch* as the hammer came back and whirled. I stuck the barrel right in his face. "Not a sound!" I said. "Not a word or I'll blow your fucking head off!"

He opened and closed his mouth, but nothing came out. I nodded at a door that seemed to lead to the back. "Open that door."

He moved, then, giving me little frightened glances as he hurried to it. He swung it open and it did, indeed, open on the back. I could see Chulo opening the back gate and letting Wilcey and Sam through. He had a peon tight around the neck with one hand and his big pistol in the other. I stepped to the door and whistled lowly. They all glanced my way and I motioned for them to come on. Then, leaving the door open, I hustled Bustamante around and shoved him through the door back out into the setting room. The servant and Martin were just as I'd left them.

I shoved Bustamante forward, then leveled down on all three of them. "Don't nobody move. Lay down on the floor!"

Martin looked as if he were going to faint and the servant just gawked at me. "Move!" I said. "On the floor! Face down!"

Bustamante was the first to react and then the others slowly followed suit, going down to their knees and then on down to lie spread-eagled on the floor.

From the floor Bustamante finally got his voice. "Senor, what is the meaning of this! What do you intend?"

"Shut your mouth! I'll tell you when you need to know."

Just then my partners came hurrying in from the kitchen. Chulo still had the boy by the neck. When he saw how I had the other prisoners, he flung him face down on the tile floor. He had the picket rope coiled over his shoulder.

"Tie these three," I said, indicating everyone except Bustamante.

Chulo commenced cutting the picket rope into handy lengths. Wilcey and Sam jerked the house servant's hands behind his back, took a good tie on them, then pulled his feet up and wrapped them.

"Tie them tight," I said.

Wilcey said, "They get away from this, they could get out of a coffin."

Martin was making whimpering sounds. I'm sure he didn't know whether to say anything or not. Finally he called softly, just as Wilcey and Sam began to tie his hands and feet. "Senor. Senor. Senor! Please!"

"Shut up, Martin."

"Please, senor, permit me to go. I have no part in this."

"You do now," I said.

Bustamante was making noises again. He said, "Senor, I demand to know the meaning of this. Are you planning to rob us? If so, take what little is here and go!"

I reached down and tapped him on the back of the head with the barrel of my revolver. I didn't do it especially hard, but it hurt from the way he winced. "Now listen, greaser," I told him, "I'm only going to instruct you one more time to keep your mouth shut. If you don't I'm going to beat your fucking face in with the barrel of this *pistola*. You *sabe* me?"

From upstairs I could hear the sound of feminine voices and I figured the Senora Bustamante, attended by her maid, was in the process of getting up. Well, she might as well get all the sleep she could. She was going to need it.

I looked around the room. There were several doors leading off besides the one to the kitchen. The first I looked into was some kind of office. It would have served, but there was a window to the outside. The next I checked on was a closet. It was big enough, but there was a bunch of stuff stored in it, wicker baskets and such. I began throwing them out the door. Sam came to help and, when we had it cleaned out, I told Wilcey and Chulo to carry our prisoners in and drop them on the floor.

"Leave Bustamante."

Then I drew Sam aside so Bustamante couldn't hear me. "Now, Sam Owl, I want you to go and do your part. Go to Bustamante senior's house and tell him that Junior requires him immediately on a matter of business importance. Tell him he must come at once. If Senior wonders why his *nino* isn't coming himself, tell him that he has some businessmen in attendance at his home and can't leave, but he begs his father to come. Now you can find the house?"

"Of course," he said.

"Speak good Mexican," I said, "and if Papa asks who you are, say you have been hired by the Senora for some special work in the house. Now take off."

He went out the front door and I turned back into the room. Wilcey and Chulo had shut our prisoners up in the closet and were standing by waiting. Bustamante was laying in the middle of the floor. I glanced up the stairs, wondering what she was doing up there, what she still looked like, if she'd recognize me, what she'd think.

The moment I'd waited a long time for was near at hand. I went over to Bustamante and nudged him with my toe. "Get up, greaser."

He got up slowly, apprehensively. But he was such a dandy that he bothered to brush off his pants and vest where they'd picked up some dust from the floor. I nudged him in the back with my gun. "Walk over there to the foot of those stairs."

I followed him, taking myself out of sight by hugging the side of the stairwell so I wouldn't be seen until someone was already down the stairs.

"Call the senora," I said.

He gave me a look. *"Perdoneme?"*

"You heard me, call the senora." I hated to say it, but I added, "Call your wife." I hated the very thought that the woman I'd loved was married to this little slicked-back dandy.

He drew himself up. "No. I will not involve my wife."

I jabbed the barrel of my revolver in his belly. He went "Oooff!" and doubled up.

From behind me Wilcey said, "Will! Goddamnit!"

"Shut up, Wilcey. It's going to get worse than that." I turned back to Bustamante. "Now call your wife or I'm going to break some of your teeth off."

He was still gasping for breath. "There is no need—" he said. "No need to involve the senora. If you mean to rob us, please do so and leave us in peace."

"Listen, goddamnit! Call your wife!"

He still didn't want to, but I made as if to poke him with my revolver and he suddenly looked up the stairs and called. "Leenda!"

There was her name. The one I'd carried around in my head for so long. Only the damn greaser couldn't say it right. He couldn't say "Linda," like it sounded; he had to say "Leenda!"

Damn him.

I stepped back beside the stairwell. "Again," I said.

He called, "Leenda! *Venga aqui.*" Come here.

I heard her voice at the top of the stairs. *"Si,* Eduardo?"

"Come down," he said. His voice had a slight tremble in it.

I could hear her steps coming down the stairs. Then she passed where I was standing and I could see the top of her head through the banister. Then she curved out of sight and I stepped out from the stairwell just as she arrived at the bottom.

"Yes, Eduardo?" she said.

She had not dressed. She was wearing a light-colored robe over what I guessed was her nightgown. She stood there looking at her husband, waiting for him to tell her why he'd called. She hadn't seen me nor Chulo nor Wilcey, who'd taken a stance against the far wall. I stepped forward and took Bustamante by the shoulder and jerked him out of the way and stood there looking at her.

She made a little sound and put her hand to her mouth. I don't know if it was because she recognized me or if it was because there was suddenly a stranger with a gun in his hand standing in front of her.

She was as beautiful as I'd remembered, maybe more so, for the woman I'd remembered had really been a girl. Now she was a woman. She stood there with her robe slightly parted so that I could see the swell of her breasts. The robe was belted at the waist and it showed her hips. Her hair was not fixed and it fell down around her shoulders, soft and natural.

I felt that taste like copper come into my throat and mouth. I said, "Did I frighten you?"

"No, I—" She took another step backwards, almost stumbling against the stairs behind her.

I had no intention of telling her who I was. Let her recognize me.

Then her husband stepped to her side, putting his arm around her. "What do you want of my wife, senor? If you mean to rob us then do so and leave! You are not a gentleman to act this way!"

Behind me Chulo and Wilcey laughed.

I said, "Don't worry about me being a gentleman. Now I want you both to sit down. Just sit down right there on that bottom step." I turned. "Chulo, go up there and fetch that woman servant. Bring her down and tie her up and put her in the closet."

He went by Bustamante and his wife, who had both sat down on the bottom step.

Linda was looking at me intently. I turned back and looked in her eyes for a long moment, then away.

Upstairs I suddenly heard a scream, then a volley of Spanish too loud for me to follow, and then Chulo appeared on the stairs with the maid slung over his shoulder like a sack of feed. He came clumping down, his teeth white in that black face of his.

Linda said, "Oh, please don't hurt her!"

"Tie her and put her in the closet," I said again.

Bustamante stood up. "I insist, senor, that you tell me what you intend!"

"You'll know soon enough," I said. "Now sit down!"

Wilcey said, "What do you think? How's it going?"

"Just fine," I answered. But I was still plenty nervous. I don't know if it was from the job or from seeing Linda again. I walked over to one of the front windows and looked out, but all I could see was the fence. I wished Sam Owl would hurry. Every minute we delayed was extending the risk. Wilcey came over to me. He glanced back at Linda. He said, quietly, "I see what you mean. About her."

I gave him a look. "Never mind that."

The sack with the thousand dollars in gold that Martin had brought was still laying in the middle of the tile floor where he'd dropped it. I kicked it over by the kitchen door. "Let's don't forget that. Senor Martin has upped the price."

Chulo was having trouble tying the maid. She was struggling and crying and cussing in Spanish. But he finally got her hog-tied, and then he and Wilcey half dragged, half carried her over to the closet door. When they opened it, there came a volley of sound that was half screaming, half begging. It was Martin.

I said to Wilcey, "Shut him up, damnit!"

"He says they're smothering. Ain't no air in that closet with the door shut."

I took a quick look at Bustamante and Linda to make sure they were still seated and weren't going anywhere and then walked over to the closet. "Martin," I said, "if you don't lay quiet and be still I'm going to let Chulo cut your ears off. You understand me?"

"Senor," he said. "Senor, please." He was talking so low that I bent down to hear him. "Senor, I want no part of this. I have no part of this. Please, please let me go. I will leave and say nothing to anyone. You keep the money. I am pleased you should have it."

"That's mighty kind of you," I said. "But I believe we'll just keep you for a while."

Then there came a knock on the door. I quickly motioned for Chulo and Wilcey to watch our captives then stole across the setting room and took a station by the door. With one hand I turned the knob and pulled it open. Senor Bustamante the senior came bustling through. "Hold it!" I said. He turned and saw me, then looked quickly around, seeing Wilcey and Chulo with guns leveled.

I'll give the old man this; he was a hell of a lot faster catching on than his son. He said, "Mother of God, bandits!"

"That's right, senor," I said. "Now get over there and lay down on your face on the floor. Tie him up, Chulo. Then sling him in the closet."

I held the door open while Sam Owl slipped through the gate and hurried inside. He had a big grin on his face.

"Any trouble?"

"Of course not," he said. He took his sombrero off and

held it in his hands. "I play the poor peon very well. I say, 'Senor, please, I am but a dumb peon come to beg your forgiveness for disturbing such a great man, but you are wanted at the casa of your son.'" He laughed. "Hell, I'm already money ahead. The old bastard gave me a peso."

They had to force Bustamante down to the floor to tie him. He was not, however, doing any talking, seeming to have the good sense to know that it would be pointless. I was watching them when I heard Sam say, "Hey!"

I looked around and Junior was breaking for the kitchen. He got through the door and into the kitchen before I could come up with him, but I caught him just as he reached for the latch to the back door. I took him by the collar and slammed him down on the floor, then jerked him up and pushed him hard against the wall. "Now listen, you little bastard, you try that again and I'll let that mean Mexican in there cut your balls off! You got me?"

He looked frightened and his carefully slicked down hair was flying all over his head. Of course he didn't know that I couldn't kill him, not just yet anyway, nor could I even mark up his face so that he'd draw attention. I shook him by the shoulders again. "You understand?"

"*Si,*" he finally said. "Yes."

"All right." Holding him by the collar I half led, half dragged him back into the parlor and flung him against a wall. Linda was standing in the middle of the room. Sam had her by one arm. I jerked my head toward where her husband was slumped on the floor. "Go and sit by your brave husband. So brave that he was going to run and leave you in the house with bandits."

She glanced at him, then at me.

"Go on," I said. "Go sit by your hero."

"That is a lie," he said. "I was going to bring help." He began to smooth his hair back with both hands.

"Sure," I said. "And how would this help have gotten in the house and what would have happened to your bride in the meanwhile? Please, answer me that!"

Linda went over and sat down on the floor beside him. Now she was looking closely at my face. I turned away. I had thought it was going to make me feel good to humiliate her and her husband by frightening them, but I wasn't taking a great deal of satisfaction out of it.

Wilcey said, "Will, hadn't we better get on with this?"

"Yeah. You're right. Time is getting short." I jerked my head toward where Bustamante was sitting. "Chulo, go bring the great bank president over here. Sam, watch the bank president's wife so that she doesn't try and leave us."

Chulo went over and jerked Bustamante up and brought him to stand in front of me. I said, "Now listen carefully, Senor El Presidente, I have a little job for you. In the company of this large gentleman who has you by the collar, you are to go to your bank before it opens and get twenty thousand dollars in gold and bring it back to me. Do you understand?"

He gave me a startled look. "I am to do what?"

I explained it to him again, patiently. "In your carriage, for that much gold will be hard to carry, even for such a giant as yourself. This *caballero,*" I indicated Chulo, "will accompany you on his horse. Only he will not go inside with you for that would perhaps make people suspicious. He does not, I don't believe, look as if he works for the bank. No, he will wait outside for you and then accompany you back to be sure no banditos can attack you along the way and steal the gold. You *sabe?*"

He straightened himself up like a little pouter pigeon. "I will do no such thing!"

"You won't, huh? I bet you will. Wilcey, you and Chulo get Papa out of the closet. Bring him out here and lay him on the floor right side up. I want his son to be able to see his face while Chulo works on him."

Over against the wall, Linda made a little snuffling sound. I looked over at her, surprised that I wasn't feeling more about seeing her again. Actually, in the course of conducting the robbery, I kept forgetting about her. If anything, I think I was feeling more curiosity to see if she actually matched up to what had been in my mind all those years.

They dragged the old man out and laid him on his back. I reckoned the position was painful, his hands tied behind his back as they were, but he never let on, just stared at the ceiling with his mouth set.

I knelt down beside him. "Now, Papa, I put a little proposition up to your son, but he won't have it. I told him to go over to the bank and bring us back some money or else I'd kill you and him and his wife. But I don't think he believes me. So in order to prove to him I'm serious I'm going to have this gentleman—" I indicated Chulo, "cut off your ear." I got up. "Chulo. Go ahead."

But the old man suddenly said, "Stop!"

"Afraid we can't," I said.

But he was looking at his son. "Go and get the money they demand."

The son said. "But, Father, it is a great sum."

"You idiot," his father said. "Do you not realize that these men are banditos and fully capable of doing what they say? Go and get the money. And be quick about it."

"But such an amount!"

"Go! The sum is not worth my life or your wife's or even yours. Now go!"

I looked at Junior. "Better mind your daddy. If you don't, we're liable to untie him and then you'd be in a hell of a lot of trouble."

The old man was still glaring at his son, probably because he hadn't left town when he was born. I said, "All right, let's get moving. We got to get this done before the town gets to stirring too much and before any bank employees can get there." I said to Junior, "Now this man, this big Mexican, will be with you. But there will be another watching both of you. If anything happens to this one, the other will come back and tell me. And if that happens I will kill both your wife and your father. If *anything* happens I will kill them. Do you understand? You are to go straight to the bank, get twenty thousand dollars, putting it in four bags, and bring it straight back to me. Chulo, see that he leaves it in the carriage and see that the carriage stays hitched." I looked back at Bustamante junior. "Now do you understand me clearly? If the police come, if anything happens to any of my men, if you tell a soul what is transpiring here, I will kill your wife and father as surely as the sun rises."

He stood there staring blankly at me until his father snapped, "Answer him!"

He ducked his head. "Yes."

"Yes, what?"

"Yes, I understand."

"You understand what?"

"I—I understand you will kill my wife and father if all does not happen as you wish."

"You have it correct."

His father said, "Do it exactly as he says. Do not be more a fool than you've always been."

"Yes, Father," he said.

I said, "Chulo, take Junior out the back and help him hitch the buggy. You stay close to him, but not too close. You might glance inside the bank after he opens the door to see that no one else is there, but don't go in."

"*Si, que no,* Weelson."

As they were going toward the kitchen I stopped Bustamante. I looked over at Linda, sitting on the floor, looking
frightened.

"You want to kiss your wife good-bye?"

He shook his head quickly.

"Might be your last chance. Anything goes wrong you
might wish you had."

"No," he said.

"Get moving, Chulo."

They went out the kitchen door and I turned back into the
room and spoke to Sam. "Go out and wait for them out
front. Follow on foot. Anything goes wrong you know what
to do. No, wait. Before you go, you and Wilcey get Senor
Bustamante here back in the closet."

They moved toward him, but he said, "No, senor, as a
favor, please do not put me back in the closet with the pig
Martin. I am disgusted hearing him crying and whining and
calling to the Mother Mary to deliver him."

Well, I don't know. I was getting to where I kind of liked
the old man. He might have been a bastard, but he was a
tough bastard. I told Wilcey and Sam to take him over
against the far wall. "Just get him out of the way. And lay
him on his side. He'll be in less of a bind that way."

"Thank you, senor," he said.

When he was moved Sam left. I stood there trying to
think if I'd forgotten anything. Wilcey said, "Will, I may be
wrong, but this damn well looks like it just might work."

I said, "I hope so."

And then I looked around at Linda. She was still slumped
against the wall, only now she was resting her face down
against one of her knees. I don't know why I was thinking
what I was about the way she'd acted. Hell, any woman
would have been afraid under the circumstances. I guess I

just hadn't expected, or at least hoped, that she wouldn't be afraid of me.

But then she didn't remember me. It was only me, the sucker, that had carried her around on my mind. I reckoned she'd never give me another thought. Well, now I was going to give her something to remember me by. And it was going to be more than just the casual hand touch we'd experienced before; the hand touch I'd remembered and remembered and never got off my mind.

"Wilcey," I said, "you go and watch the front door. Get there by that front window."

"All right," he said. He moved across the room.

I turned to Linda, my throat tight. "Get up," I said. I was talking to her now like I talked to women; not like I spoke to a mind's dream.

She looked up. *"Perdoneme?"*

"You heard me. Get up."

She looked a long time into my face and then she arose, slowly, reluctantly. When she was standing she stood there, her hands at her side, looking fearful.

"Go upstairs," I told her.

"Perdoneme?"

"Goddamnit! You heard me! Get upstairs."

She turned and started for the stairs, casting little glances over her shoulder at me.

I turned to follow her. From the window Wilcey said, "Will?"

"What?"

"What you got in mind?"

"You care?" She had taken three steps up the stairs and I was at the foot. She was looking back. Both at me and at Wilcey.

"Get up there!" I said to her. "Go up to your bedroom."

"Will?"

"Shut up, Wilcey."

"It ain't your style."

"What do you know about my style. Goddamn you, shut up. You just watch out that front window."

Linda still paused, uncertain. "Goddamnit," I said. "Get on up there." I started up the steps.

Wilcey called to me. "I know all about it, Will. But this ain't the way. Not at pistol point."

I shouted down at him. "You go to hell!"

"I probably am. But I be goddamned if I want to listen to you a bunch of nights after you do something you'll be sorry for later."

Our voices were echoing off the stone walls and the tile floor. Above me Linda had clutched her robe around her and turned to face me at the top of the stairs.

"Listen, Wilcey," I yelled, "you just watch that goddamn front door and don't worry about what I'm doing! You hear me! Goddamn, you sound like Les Richter, and that's the last man I vowed would ever play at conscience for me. Now do your job! We're robbing a bank!"

"What are you robbing, Will?"

"Go to hell!"

She still stood there, trembling in that light-colored lavender robe. I felt savage, angry, made more so by Wilcey reminding me of who I was.

He said, "All right," with a kind of resigned tone in his voice, and I could see him turn and look out the window.

She was at the landing at the top of the stairs. I said, "Woman, get on up. Go to your bedroom."

She didn't move until I came up to her, just stood there clutching her robe around her. I took her by the arm. "Which is your bedroom?"

She moved reluctantly. "Senor, what do you intend?"

"Just what you think," I said. I pulled her along the

hallway. At the end a door was open. I looked inside. It was a big, light, airy room with a big feather bed along one side. I pushed her through the door and stepped in. The bed was so soft you could still see the impressions their bodies had left when they slept. I took it all in, contrasting their bedroom with all the places I'd slept, all the cheap hotels, all the nights on the prairie.

She'd moved a little away from me. I looked at her. I said, "So we meet again."

"I do not understand, senor."

"Maybe you do and maybe you don't. First time I met you was at your uncle's, in Villa Union. I was posing as a cattle buyer then, but I wasn't no cattle buyer. Me and my partners had just robbed a bank on the Texas side. Then I followed you here to Sabinas Hidalgo and had dinner at your daddy's ranch outside of town here. I was posing as a man who was fixing to start a horse ranch here in Mexico. But I wasn't. Me and my partners had just robbed a bank in Uvalde, Texas, and I'd personally killed three men. Now this time I stand before you as what I really am, a bandito. An outlaw. Which is what I've always been. But you still don't remember me?"

She shook her head slowly.

"I wondered if you would," I said. "When I was planning this robbery, I wondered if you'd know me when we met."

"Why have you come to this town to rob this bank? Why here?"

"To see you," I said. "To get you out of my mind once and for all. I've carried you in my head ever since that day in your uncle's house. I kept robbing, hoping to get enough money to present myself as a respectable businessman and to court you and marry you. But then when I had gained the money and had come to Sabinas for that purpose I was too late. You were already married." My voice got an edge in it.

"To the brave and upstanding Senor Eduardo Bustamante the junior."

"I do not understand all of this, senor." Some of the fright was going out of her face and I could well understand why. She thought I was talking to her of love which made her think she had a leg up on the situation.

"I'm sure you don't, you little cold-hearted bitch. It has been my misfortune to have always been taken by bad women. I would have to say you have been the worst."

"I—I do not understand of what you speak." The fright was back in her face again, as I'd intended. "Senor, I have never seen you before in my knowledge and I do not know why you speak so to me."

"A touch. That's what I've had in my head for all these years. Just the touch of our hands and you don't even remember. Why should I remember? Why should I have been the sucker? Why should I have been risking my life to get money to court you and marry you? When you didn't even remember. You don't remember the touch, do you?"

"No, I— No, senor, I do not remember you at all. And I understand none of this."

"It was the night I came to supper at your daddy's ranchero. You sat across from me and you looked at me all through the meal. Your father and I talked, but you and I looked at each other. When the meal was over you made it so that you and I would be the last to leave the room, and in the hall that led into the parlor, you reached out with your hand to mine. It was but the smallest touch, yet it has never left my hand. It has kept me from being with good women—women who cared for me."

"I'm sorry, senor. But how can I know of this?"

"Well," I said, "I can see that. So this time I'm going to leave you with something you will remember. This time I'm going to be sure that you won't forget me. This time it will not just be me who is doing the remembering. This time you will remember."

"What do you mean, senor?" She put her hand to her mouth. The other arm was clutched across her chest, covering her breasts.

"Just what you think. Take off your clothes."

I don't know why the shock should have come over her face as it did. She was a grown woman and she should have known what I'd brought her to the bedroom for.

But she'd turned white. She said, "Senor, I implore you. *Por favor,* I understand the robbing. You are a bandito. But would you do this? Have you no honor?"

"Listen," I said, "what I haven't got is a hell of a lot of time. Your husband should be back here pretty pronto. Now get them goddamn clothes off."

"No! No!" She backed up until she ran into the wall. There she stood, one hand to her mouth, the other folded across her breasts. I walked to her. "Take them off or I'll rip them off. You understand?"

"Senor . . . No, please! My husband's father is downstairs. I will be shamed the rest of my life. I have done nothing to deserve this. Please."

I reached out and jerked her arm away from her breasts. Then with my other hand, I took her robe and gown in a clutch and ripped them down the front. She cringed against the wall, trying to pull the shreds of her clothes back around her. I jerked her hands away and then pulled the rags off her shoulders. They fell down around her feet and she stood there naked.

My God, she was beautiful. Just almost perfectly beautiful. I looked at her for a second and then she fell to her knees, clutching her hands together at her breasts. She was sobbing now, just crying quietly, not making any big fuss about it.

Well, Wilcey was right. It wasn't my style. The copper taste was all gone out of my mouth and the tightness out of my throat.

I left her sagged down on the floor and walked over and looked out the big, double windows. There was nothing but open fields beyond. She could yell out and scream for help until she turned blue in the face and no one would hear her.

I turned and started out of the room, but stopped at the door and looked back at her. She had her head down, still crying. I said, "You reckon you'll remember me now?"

She didn't answer, just went on crying and I went down the stairs. Wilcey was still at the front window. He turned as I hit the landing.

"See anything?" I asked him.

He shook his head and continued looking at me. Finally he said, "That was fast."

"Not for a little talk. Especially if you don't have that much to talk about."

"That all you did? Talk?"

"Aw, go to hell, Wilcey. You ain't got to know everything."

He turned back to looking out the window. "I didn't think it was your style."

I didn't answer him, just went over to where Bustamante the elder was laying against the wall. His face was drawn and tight and I could imagine the way he was hog-tied was beginning to hurt pretty bad. I said, "I'm sorry, senor, but I cannot untie you. You can understand that."

He nodded, a brief jerk of his head.

"However, your son should be back soon and then we will be gone."

"I understand," he said.

I checked inside the closet. Our prisoners were breathing heavy but none of them seemed to have suffocated. The fat maid was making little moaning sounds, and Martin sounded as if he were sobbing. He turned his head just enough to see me. "Senor, for the love of God! Please, please, release me! Have I cheated you? Have I not been fair?"

"Martin, if you don't shut your goddamn mouth, I'm going to kick it in. I don't like you, Martin, or anything about you. And you'll be lucky if I don't kill you before we leave."

From the window I heard Wilcey calling me. I stepped back in the living room. Wilcey said, "Will, Sam just came through the gate door."

I went over and unbolted the big front door and the little half-breed came slipping through. He was wearing a big grin.

"How'd it go, Sam?"

He snapped his fingers. "No trouble. They must have the money for Chulo had a big smile on his face and El Presidente didn't look any too happy. They ought to just about be turning into the back now."

"Good. Go out and help Chulo get Bustamante in here. And don't forget to bring in the gold. Let's be sure Senor Bustamante knows how to count."

"Exactly," Sam said. He went out through the door to the kitchen.

Wilcey said, "You want me to stay at the window?"

"Yeah."

A moment later Sam and Chulo came in, the big Mexican shoving Bustamante in front of him. Sam had two sacks and Bustamante was carrying another two. I told them to drop it in the middle of the floor. "Throw Bustamante over against that wall by his daddy."

I went over and knelt down and opened the sacks. It was gold all right. I wasn't going to take time to count, but it looked close enough to $20,000 to suit me. I stood up. "All right. It's here. Let's go to making plans to get the hell out of here. Chulo, tie up El Presidente there. And tie him damn good and tight. Sam, you go watch out the back door." I took a step toward the stairs and then stopped. "No, Sam," I said. "First go upstairs and bring down the senora."

Wilcey was looking over at me. "Damnit, Wilcey," I said, "keep watching out that window."

I watched Chulo tying up Bustamante. He was none too gentle. Then Sam appeared at the head of the stairs, holding Linda by one arm, pushing her ahead of him. She was not resisting, but she was coming reluctantly. She had changed to some kind of gray dress, very loose fitting, very drab. They came down the stairs and I stopped and picked up a piece of rope laying on the floor. "All right, Sam," I said, "go and watch out the back door."

I motioned to Linda. "Get over here."

She came toward me, her head down, her hands clasped in front of her. From the window Wilcey said, "Will, you want me to do that?"

"Hell no," I said. I told Linda. "Lay down on your face and put your hands behind you."

She did, moving very slowly. There looked to be the tracks of tears on her face.

I knelt beside her and pulled her hands together. Then I stopped. She was going to have to be tied tight and I wasn't sure I could do that. Chulo was finished with Bustamante and I waved him over. "Tie her up, Chulo," I said. "And make damn sure she can't get loose."

I turned and walked away as the big Mexican came over, his teeth gleaming in his face. "I do it good," he said.

"Sure, you do that."

I walked over and stood by Wilcey and looked out the front window. He gave me a quick glance. I did not turn to watch Chulo tying Linda, not even when I heard a sharp little cry from her.

From against the wall, Bustamante junior said, "Senor, you will regret this. That I promise you."

"Not as much as you're going to," I told him.

Wilcey said, "Will, it looks like it's going pretty good."

"We ain't out of here yet," I said.

I turned toward them. Chulo was standing up. Linda was laying on her face, her hands and feet almost pulled together behind her back. I walked over to her. She was crying quietly. I knelt down beside her. "I think now you'll remember me. The name is Wilson Young. Wilson Young. Can you remember that?"

But before she could answer, Wilcey called from the window. "Will, come quick. There are men outside the gate. They look like *Federales.*"

SEVEN

I rushed to the window. Through it I could see that the fence gate was open, and through that, I could see men and horses moving back and forth. Occasionally I caught a glimpse of the gray uniforms of the federal police, the *Federales*.

I never even paused. I just whirled and ran into the kitchen and to the back door where Sam was. He hadn't seen anything. "Sam," I said, "the police are out there. Run quick, while I cover you, and get our rifles off our horses in the stables. Hurry!"

I crouched in the doorway, my revolver in my hand, while he ran into the stable. There was no movement that I could see, but of course the fence was high enough to shield my view and the back gate was closed.

In a moment he was back, running awkwardly over the little space from the stable with four rifles cradled in his arms. I grabbed three from him. "Put one in the chamber,"

I told him, "and watch this back way. I'll be back to tell you what's going on."

Then I ran into the parlor. I pitched a rifle to Chulo, one to Wilcey, and kept one myself.

"All right," I said. "We got troubles. But we'll get out of here somehow."

Wilcey said, "It don't look good, Will."

"Hell, it don't. Only thing I can't figure out is how they got on to us."

From the side of the room Bustamante junior began to laugh. He said, "I told you you would regret this, senor. Now we will see who is correct."

I took two steps toward him. "What do you mean?"

Laying on his belly as he was with his hands and feet strapped like a mud dauber's nest, he had to work to turn his head toward me. He said, "It is my pleasure to inform you that it is I, Eduardo Bustamante, the president of the bank, who has brought the officers of the law down on you."

"Oh, shit!" I said. "What do you mean?"

"I will tell you that I left a note for an employee that I knew would be at the bank very early, giving him instructions to send the *Federales* to my house. And now, as you see, they have arrived." His voice was triumphant, full of itself.

The damn fool.

I just stood there, feeling myself go tired inside, letting my revolver dangle at the end of my arm.

I walked slowly over to where he was laying and stood there staring down at him. "You damn fool," I said. "You dumb sonofabitch. Do you have any idea what you've done?"

"I have foiled you, senor! As I warned. You will not escape here."

"Oh, shit," I said. I felt like kicking his face in. The dumb bastard had put me in a bind like I'd never been in before. I said, "Don't you know that we'd have been gone by now and you all would have been safe? That all you'd have lost would have been the money? Now you are going to lose a great deal more."

A little further down the wall, where he lay on his side, his father said, softly, sadly, *"Eduardo, idioto. Usted es un idioto!"*

He didn't even bother to use the familiar *tu* to his own son, but, instead, used the formal *usted* to tell his son what an idiot he had been.

I squatted down beside him. "You are truly a fool. You think we are trapped. Yes, of course we are trapped, but so are you. We are wanted men. Every one of us has a price on his head. None of us will surrender for all we can expect will be a hanging or a firing squad. So we will not be taken alive. We have nothing to lose. But before we die, you will be killed, your wife will be killed, your father will be killed, your servants will be killed, and some of the men outside attacking us will be killed. You see, we are very experienced gunmen and it is going to take a great deal of effort to kill us. No, senor, you have made a mistake. You are a damn fool."

I stood up. "Chulo, you and Wilcey pull the prisoners out of the closet and put them in the middle of the room. Then pull Don Bustamante and his idiot son into the middle of the room. Wilcey, I'll watch your post while you do that."

I went to the window and broke out the glass with the end of my rifle and squatted down.

Actually the house was very well set up for a defense. There were bars over the windows and there weren't that many windows on the ground floor. In the parlor we had the front window, which I was at, and then windows to my left. There were none to the right, just stone walls. I had not seen any in the back. And then there was the high fence that would have to be negotiated under fire if the outside forces wished to rush the house. The doors were heavy and of oak. They wouldn't give easily and I doubted if they could be fired through.

Chulo and Wilcey had finished pulling all of the prisoners into the middle of the room. "Chulo," I said, "you go and relieve Sam. I want you at the back."

After me he was the second best gunman of us all. "Tell Sam to come in here."

I left the window. "Wilcey, take the front. Shoot anyone who shows anything to shoot at."

I walked over to the clump of bodies in the middle of the room. Bustamante the junior was on the outside, toward the wall with the window. His father was below him. His wife was a few feet away, turned on her side, facing away. I came up to him. I said, "Now, El Presidente, let me tell you what your heroism and intelligence has done. Very soon they will be firing through these windows. The walls are of stone and there will be a great many ricochets bouncing all over this room. My friends and I will be laying on the floor against the walls. The ricochets will not hit us. But they will hit you and your wife and your father and your servants. We will not have to kill you. The people you have sent to save you will do that."

From nearby his father was saying, softly, *"Idioto, idioto, idioto!"*

I got up and, with my boots, shoved the bags of gold over to where Bustamante the junior could see them. "Look closely, my friend. Study them. That is what you're about to die for."

Then I took him by the cord between his feet and hands, causing him to cry out, and dragged him a few feet further up. "And look there. There is your wife. I want you to be able to see her when the bullets start coming through the windows."

She was crying softly and with pain. I knelt down beside her. "Why are you crying? You have what you want. Can any woman want more than to die by her husband's side?"

"Ah, senor," she said. "Please. Please, please. My hands and my feet hurt so. Please."

I stood up. "You want to talk to me, don't call me 'senor,' call me by the name I told you was mine. I don't want you to forget me again."

Sam had come in. He stood there, his rifle in his hand, watching me. I pointed at the side windows. "Over there, Sam. Shoot anything you can see. Ain't no friends outside."

Bustamante the senior said, "Senor, I would speak with you."

I turned toward the window where Wilcey was stationed. "Not now, Don Bustamante. I think I already know what you've got in mind, but I've got to study on it."

He said, with difficulty, for his face was pressed against the tile floor. "I feel this is urgent that we speak. There is no use in so many people being killed over my son's foolish mistake."

"Not yet, Don Bustamante. Perhaps I want your son to be shown for the fool he is."

I walked on over to stand by Wilcey's side. I wasn't going to explain what I meant by that, but I hoped that Linda had heard.

Wilcey said, "Kind of looking bad, ain't it, Will?"

"Not yet," I said. "You watch close. I'll be right back."

Then I turned and crossed the room swiftly and went upstairs. I went through the door of Linda's bedroom and to the window. There was a gang of the *Federales* in their gray uniforms milling around. Out beyond them, staring on with curiosity were a line of peons in their white pants tied at the ankles and their straw sombreros. There was one *Federale* on his horse who was obviously the *jefe*, the head man. He was riding back and forth directing his troops into a single line around the outside of the wall.

With the barrel of my rifle I broke out the pane of glass and eased the end through. The leather straps that crossed across his chest made a perfect target. He was wearing one of those new fangled caps with a shiny bill across it. I cocked my rifle, sighting on the center of his chest. He'd stopped his horse and was yelling at someone, pointing where they should go. All I had to do was squeeze the trigger and he was a dead man.

Then I slowly eased the hammer down with my thumb and got up and went downstairs. Just as I hit the landing Wilcey's rifle rang out.

"Yeah?" I asked him.

"Sonofabitch stuck his head through the gate. I think I hit him."

"Well, hold up," I said. "Let me think."

A volley of shots suddenly broke out from the back. It sounded like Chulo was doing a little business. Then a bullet crashed through the side window and whined around the walls. It wouldn't take much more of that until we had no prisoners to barter with.

"Don Bustamante?"

"*Si?*"

"Do you know the men who are outside? The *Federales?*"

"Yes, of course."

"Will they listen to you?"

"Yes. I have much authority in this region. I know the *Capitan* very well."

Several shots suddenly crashed through the side window and went ricocheting all over the room. Sam fired back. He said, "One got his head over the wall. I don't believe he'll do that anymore."

I crawled on my hands and knees over to Don Busta-mante's side and got out my pocketknife and began cutting his bonds. "It worries me, senor," I told him, "that those men are foolish enough to shoot in here without knowing what they'll hit. Are you sure they'll act under your orders?"

"Yes," he said. He sat up, groaning slightly and rubbing his wrists.

"It'll take a minute for the blood to come back. Your idiot son got any brandy here?"

"I think," he said, "in that cabinet."

I scuttled across the room and fetched up in front of a mahogany cabinet. It was full of all kinds of liquor. I found a bottle of brandy and hustled back over to the Don with it.

He took a drink, sighing, and then I had a pull. It was damn good stuff. Better than I was used to. I called, "Wilcey!" He turned and I pitched him the bottle. Then I sat down by the Don. "Now let us go over this very carefully for all our lives depend on it. Do you understand that?"

He shrugged. "Of course. Do not judge the father by the son."

"A good point," I said. I got out a cigarillo and lit it. I said, "You must impress upon the *Capitan* that we are desperate men, that we will not be taken alive. That we know if we are, that it will only be a matter of hours before we are shot or hanged. So we would have nothing to gain by surrendering. And impress upon him that we will not die alone. That you and your family and servants and Martin will die also."

He made a slight face at the mention of Martin. "Perhaps the cost would be worth it," he said.

"Not right now, senor. Martin will be dealt with later. For

now you must impress upon the *Federales* that we are very experienced *pistoleros* and that some of them will die also. Do you understand?"

"Of course, senor. It is clear that you are what you say. No, they will believe me."

"But will they obey?"

"I would think so. After all, I have much authority here."

"But they are very excitable men. That they would shoot through the windows without knowing the consequences does not give me a great deal of confidence."

"I am certain they will obey me."

"I hope," I said, "for your sake that you're right. Now. Tell them they must withdraw. Once they are completely away from here we will be going out the back. All of you will be going with us. We are going to walk. You and your party will be on the outside. Me and my friends will be on the inside. If a single shot is fired you will all be killed immediately." From the window Wilcey glanced back at me. There was nothing in his expression. He knew I was running a bluff.

Senor Bustamante nodded. "I understand."

"The *Federales* are not to follow. When we have gone two or three miles and are out on the prairie and have a good chance to outrun the pursuit, then you will be released. If no one interferes, no one will be hurt. Is that clear?"

"That is clear. And you will release us? Unharmed."

"Senor, I am a robber, not a killer. You will be released when I'm convinced we can make our escape."

He searched my face for a long moment. Then he nodded. "Very well, I will tell the *Capitan* that I believe you. And that they are not to interfere in any way. Is it acceptable that they will pursue you after we are released?"

I had to smile a little at that. "Why yes, Don, I reckon that will have to be acceptable since I'll have no way to stop them once I let y'all go."

"Very well." He stood up. "I will go now and tell them."

Together we hurried over to the big front door. Fortunately no more shots had come through the window. "Now be careful," I said. "Those trigger-happy sonofabitches out there are liable to shoot you before you can get a word said."

I cracked the door a little and called out, *"Cuidado!"* A shot immediately rang out and a bullet smacked into the heavy door. *"Alto!"* I yelled. "Hold your fire. *Es Senor Bustamante!"*

The Don got around to my side and stuck his head out the door a few inches. In Spanish he called out that he was coming out and that they were not to fire. After a second a voice yelled back something I couldn't hear. The Don nodded. "That is *Capitan* Flores. I will go out now."

"I hope they understand," I said.

"They will."

He went down the walk and then disappeared through the gate. I bolted the door and went over and squatted by Wilcey.

"What do you think?" I asked him.

He shrugged. "What else can we do?"

"We could break and run for it."

"Shit! I know them Mexicans can't shoot, but as many as are probably out there they'd have a hell of a hard time missing."

"He'll be a few minutes. I'm going to go check on Chulo. Call me if he gets back before I do."

I turned and ran quickly into the kitchen. Chulo was squatting by the half-opened door. He was using his pistol.

"How's it going, Nigger?"

He gave me a huge grin. "Very well, *amigo*. They come

through the gate once. I shoot one of them. They don't come no more."

I patted him on the shoulder. "We'll be going pretty soon. With the gold."

"Aaah," he said. "The gold."

"Plenty of gold," I said. I turned and went back in the parlor and up to Wilcey at the window. "Anything doing?"

"Not yet," he said. He looked sideways at me. "What are you going to do if the old man don't come back?"

"He'll come back."

"What if he don't?"

"He wouldn't leave his son and daughter-in-law in here."

"I don't know—He don't seem all that fond of his son."

"Com'on, Wilcey," I said. "Quit worrying so damn much. That old Don ain't the kind of a man to run out on his people. Whether he likes them or not. I swear, sometimes you can act like the worst old lady I ever saw."

Behind me someone in the heap of bodies was moaning softly. I imagine they were wishing more than anyone that the *Federales* would cooperate. I yelled at Bustamante, "Hey, Senor Presidente, I am sure by now you are very happy you told *la policia*. I am sure you are enjoying yourself very much."

He didn't answer, but his wife did. She said, softly, "Senor Young. Senor Young! Please!"

I walked over and squatted down beside her. "Ah," I said, "so you remember my name. Do you remember anything else?"

"Please, senor," she said. She was sweating and her hair was plastered against her forehead. "Please, senor, I am in much pain. Please loosen the ropes. My hands have gone numb."

"Sorry, senora," I said. "You wouldn't have me treat you any different than the others, would you? If I turned you loose I'd have to do it for the rest. Remember you are a great lady. You are married to the bank president."

"Senor . . ." Her voice was getting weaker. "Please."

"No," I said.

Her tongue came out and licked her lips and it occurred to me that they might all be getting thirsty. But she said, "Senor, please. Lean closer so I may whisper."

"All right." I leaned down and put my ear near her lips, about half expecting her to bite it. But she said, "If you will untie me, we can go back upstairs. This time I will remember you."

Well, I was that shocked. I started to laugh. This was the lady of my dreams, the perfect lady? Ready to give herself just because of a little pain. I don't know why, but somehow, it didn't surprise me. I whispered in her ear, "But senora, with your husband downstairs? Would that be proper?"

"I don't care about my husband," she said. "He is a little worm."

I looked across to her husband. "Hey, El Presidente, your wife just called you a little worm."

"That is nothing," she said. "I have told him as much."

From the window, Wilcey called me. "Will, why don't you cut the women's hands loose. They got to be hurting pretty bad." He was frowning at me.

"Yes, senor," she said. "Please. Just the hands. I have much pain in my shoulders."

"Well," I said, "okay. But anybody tries to make trouble, they're going to get killed."

I took out my knife and cut the cord between her feet and hands. She sagged forward with a sigh. Then I cut the bonds around her wrists.

She said, "Ooohhh."

Then I went over to her maid and cut hers. She didn't make a sound, and for a second I thought she'd passed out.

But then her eyes fluttered open. After I cut the cords around her wrists she immediately sat up and began stretching. I imagined she'd been hurting worse than the senora, but she wasn't lady enough to know it.

"Wilcey?"

"What?"

"No sign of the Don yet?"

He shook his head. "And it's been awhile. They ain't got that much to talk about."

I got up and went in the kitchen and found a jug of water. I brought it back and gave her a glance and went over and squatted down by Wilcey.

I got out a cigarillo and lit it. "Don't worry," I said. "This place won't be that tough to defend. If worse comes to worse we'll move upstairs, and it'll take more than that sorry bunch of play soldiers out there to take us. I bet there ain't twenty of them."

Wilcey said, dryly, "You want to bet that somebody ain't on the way right now to bring more help?"

The jug of brandy was sitting on the floor and I uncorked it and had a good pull. I looked over at Sam, crouching at his window. "You doing all right, Owl?"

"*Esta bueno,*" he said, without turning.

Well, I was starting to get a little nervous myself. I said to Wilcey, "You reckon that old man knows I'm bluffing about killing them?"

"I don't know," Wilcey said. "*I* know you're bluffing. But then I know you. Let me think what would be on my mind if I was in the old man's place." He looked out the window, biting his lower lip, thinking. Finally he said, "I don't know. You play act pretty well. Naw, hell, I know your goddamn style too well. Though you did like to have fooled the hell out of me when you took that woman upstairs. What the hell was in your mind to pull a stunt like that? Was you trying to scare her?"

"No," I said. "I meant to do what I took her upstairs for."

"But you didn't."

"Goddamnit, you don't know what I did!"

"You wasn't up there that long."

I looked out the window a long moment. Finally I said, "Well, sometimes a man tries to do something that ain't in his style. For a little while he maybe thinks he can do it. But finally it gets to feeling so wrong he ain't got no choice, but to see he can't do it. Then he don't do it."

Wilcey said, looking out the window, "Where is that old sonofabitch! Goddamn, I'm commencing to get a little nervous."

As was I. But it wasn't going to do any good to tell Wilcey that. In my mind I resolved that if the old man didn't show up in the next couple of minutes we were going to make a break for it. Every little bit of time that went by only gave them more time to get prepared or to figure out how to come and get us. In my mind's eye I could see the old Don and this *Capitan* squatting in the dust while the Don drew out exactly where we were and how we were fixed.

I looked over my shoulder. The water had revived our prisoners enough where they were starting to mumble. Linda was still sitting with her head down and her hands folded in her lap, but I could see the maid picking at the cords around her feet. "*Mujer!*" I yelled. "No! *Alto!*" I pulled my revolver and cocked and pointed it at her. She got a frightened look on her face and immediately lay flat on her back.

Well, I was really getting nervous. I stood up. "Wilcey, we better start figuring a way to get out of here. I'm going to check out the back and—"

He said, "The gate's opening."

I whirled and dropped down beside him, and sure enough, it was the old Don coming through. He had his hands up and he paused, just long enough for us to recognize him and then came on. I jumped over to the door and unbolted it. I looked over at Wilcey, waiting. He nodded, and I opened the door a crack, waiting for the pressure of the old man's hands before swinging it far enough open for him to enter.

He came in, looking I couldn't tell what. Old, I guess. At first I hadn't thought of him being that old, but he seemed to have aged as the day had gone along. Now he looked seventy years old.

I took him by the arm and took him over by the wall near Wilcey's window and eased him down on the floor. "Let's have a drink first," I said. Wilcey pitched me the bottle and I had a pull and then offered it to him. He declined, shaking his head.

"Suit yourself," I said. Then I put the cork in the bottle and set it beside me. "Well, what do they say?"

He was panting slightly. "They say they will do as you demand."

"Do you believe them?"

"Yes. They are under my orders."

"What took so long, then?"

He hesitated a long moment before answering. "It was some difficulty with the *jefe* of the *policia*. He is a political man and he is aligned with Martin." He jerked his head toward our prisoners. "He thinks he can become of importance in this matter."

"But the *Capitan* of the *Federales* overruled him?"

He straightened slightly. "No, senor. I overcame him."

"Can he be trusted?"

He paused just a little too long to suit me. Finally he said, "Yes, I think so."

I said, "But if he is a political ally of Martin's, wouldn't it be to his advantage for you to be killed."

He looked down at his hands. "Yes."

I nodded. "That's what I thought." I fumbled in my shirt and got out a cigarillo and lit it. "Senor, how many men do they have out there?"

He thought a moment. "About twenty I would think."

"How many are of the *jefe de policia*?"

He shook his head. "Very few."

I sat there smoking for a second. I asked, "Had they started to withdraw as you left?"

"No. But they had promised."

I thought a moment more. "I want you to go back out there and talk to them again. I want you to tell them they are to withdraw up to the plaza. They are to fire a gun when they have done so. A single shot. Tell them I am going to come out with one of you to see that they have withdrawn. Tell them I will not be fooled. And tell them that I say again they are not to get within several miles of me as we leave."

He heaved a sigh. "Ah, senor, I will be glad when this business is finished. I am an old man."

"Thank your son for this," I said.

He said, "Perhaps a drink of the brandy first."

I handed him the bottle and he had a pull and then we went to the door. We yelled out at them and then he took a deep breath and went out.

I shut the door and bolted it. "Watch," I told Wilcey. "I'm going to the back."

First I stopped by to see how Sam was doing. He didn't look as if everything was as funny as he usually found it. His face looked kind of drawn. He said, "We go pretty soon?"

"Pretty soon," I said.

"You don't tell me it's going to be like this."

I patted him on the shoulder. "Think of all the gold and how we'll spend it."

"Maybe," he said.

I got up, stopped by where Wilcey was long enough to grab up the bottle of brandy, tell him to watch the two women, and then went on out to the kitchen. Chulo was at the door, though he was sitting. I handed him the bottle of brandy and he gave me that big tooth grin in his black face and uncorked the bottle. "Ah, *amigo*," he said, "I thenk you have forgotten me."

"Go to hell, Nigger," I said.

He took a long drink, breathed out, and said, "How it look, *amigo?*"

"Goddamn bad," I said.

He flashed his teeth again. "Good. Maybe we get to kill a lot of them goddamn *Federales*. It will help the nation of Mexico if we do so."

I laughed. As tense as things were it was good to talk to Chulo. He never worried about anything. I said, "What you think, Chumacho? You think we get away with all the money and go and get drunk and fuck all the women in Mexico?"

"Why not, *amigo?* Do not we deserve it? Are we not good men?"

I laughed again. "That is very correct, my black-hearted friend. Tell me, can they keep us here? Can they stop us?"

"Only if they no longer wish to live to eat the avocado and drink pulque."

"I could not agree more." I stood up. "Don't let them in the back. We will be leaving very shortly."

He was looking out the door. "It will make them very sad. Our leaving."

"They'll probably cry," I said.

And then I was gone, out the door and into the parlor.

I went up to Martin, taking out my pocketknife as I did, and cut his bonds. He went spread-eagled on the floor, moaning softly. I nudged him with my boot. "Go to collecting yourself. Me and you is going to take a little walk shortly."

Wilcey said, "He's coming back."

I went to the door, unlocked it, and let him in. When we were both settled against the wall I asked, "Well?"

He nodded, seemingly out of breath. "They agree. The *Capitan* says he will fire a single shot when they reach the square."

"And they know not to get too close when we are withdrawing?"

"Yes. They say they will follow so far back you will not be able to see them."

"All right." I got up and jerked Martin to his feet. He looked like he was going to need two or three handkerchiefs as soaked with sweat as he was. He could barely stand, his legs were so cramped. Holding him by the arm, I walked him around a little until he seemed to be navigating better.

"What are you going to do?" Wilcey asked me.

"Have a look around outside with Mister Martin for protection. Make damn sure they have really withdrawn."

Wilcey said, "Will, why don't you let me or Sam or Chulo do that?"

Just then I heard the sound of the single gunshot. I said, "Why?"

He hesitated and then said, "Because if anything happens to you it more than likely means the finish of all of us. I hate to see you go out there."

"Don't be a damn fool," I said. "They ain't going to shoot at me. Now you get busy and cut the ropes on the rest of these people. Get them on their feet and moving around. They're fixing to do some walking."

I got Martin by the collar and went over and unlocked the front door and opened it. Then I taken out my revolver and cocked it and put it against the back of his head. "Now listen, greaser, me and you is fixing to take a little walk outside. You so much as blink your eyes the wrong way and I'm going to blow your fucking head off. Now move out through that door."

Well, he was dazed by all that had happened to him. He'd quit whining, he'd quit begging, he'd even quit talking. As we went out I said to Wilcey, "Better bolt this door, just in case."

"You be careful out there."

We marched from the house to the gate. I opened it and stepped through, Martin in front of me. I looked around, carefully letting my eyes rove over every building. Fortunately, we were at the outskirts and there were not many houses. And fortunately, Mexicans don't like bushes and trees that much, so there was very few places of conceal- ment. I looked up the dusty street that led to the plaza, but I couldn't see anything. I started walking sideways to my right, Martin in front of me, the fence at my back. We went slowly as I carefully looked for any sign of movement. There was none.

We went down the right side of the fence, across the back, and then up the other side. Only when I was near the front again, did I see anything. There was an adobe ruin just off to the left of Bustamante's house a hundred yards. The roof had fallen in, but some of the walls were still standing, and as we turned the corner at the front of the fence, I caught a glint of sunlight flashing off something shiny, like a rifle barrel. I took a quick look and saw movement. I took a firmer grip on Martin's collar and hustled him up the fence and through the gate. Wilcey had the door open when we got to it. I went inside and told Bustamante, "Don, they've left some men up here in that old adobe out there. You go out there and yell at that *Capitan* to get them the hell out of there."

We went back out the door, and while I hung back, Don Bustamante went through the gate and yelled in Spanish to the *Federales Capitan*. In a moment a man on a horse came trotting down the street from the plaza. About halfway down he pulled up and yelled something at the ruined little adobe house. Pretty soon three men in the gray uniforms of the *Federales* came slipping out carrying their rifles. They set off at a trot toward the plaza.

"All right," I said, pulling Don Bustamante back inside. "Maybe they'll play it straight from now on."

When we got in the door the prisoners were up and milling around. They didn't look that much worse for wear. Linda raised her head when I came through the door, but then she looked away.

"Sam," I said. "Take the gold out and split it up amongst our saddlebags. Make sure the horses are all cinched up tight. And hurry, we got to start moving." I turned to Wilcey. "We're going out through the kitchen and then out the back door."

Pushing the prisoners ahead of us, we went into the kitchen. I had Wilcey hold them there while Chulo and I went out to the stable. Sam had the gold loaded and was in the process of checking cinch straps. "Let's lead these horses out of here, Chulo. Sam, take the buggy out."

I went back in the house and Wilcey and I herded the prisoners out into the backyard. Now that we were all out in the open like that I was really in a hurry. I didn't know for sure what them damn *Federales* were liable to do. All Mexicans are excitable, but Mexicans with guns and the right to shoot them are the worst of all. Far as I knew that goddamn *Capitan* might take it in his head that it would be to his greater glory and honor to lose a few of our prisoners in order to capture or kill me and my partners. So I wanted to get us shaped up and moving as fast as possible.

As Sam and Chulo came out leading the horses and the buggy, I said to Wilcey, "Listen, Chulo and I are going out through the small gate and have a look around. If it's all clear, you open that big gate and then bring everyone through. Lead the horses and you and Sam get in the middle. Put the prisoners in a circle on the outside of the horses. Maybe that will keep them trigger-happy Mexicans from shooting." I turned to Chulo. "Get Martin by the neck and keep him in front of you. You and I are going to have a look around outside." I went over to Don Bustamante. "Come, senor. Stay in front of me. We're going outside."

There were two gates in the back, a little one for people and a big double one for the buggy and such. With Don Bustamante in front of me, I went out the small one first, cutting to my left, my pistol drawn and cocked, holding it over the Don's shoulder. Chulo came out right behind me, holding Martin by the collar. I looked, but I didn't see anything. "All right, Wilcey," I yelled, "let's give it a try."

I could hear them throwing down the heavy plank that held the double doors closed, and then they were coming through. Wilcey and Sam were in the middle, each leading two horses. Wilcey was also leading the buggy horse, the buggy trailing. The prisoners were on the outside in the best circle Wilcey could arrange them in.

I told Chulo, "Put that sonofabitch on the outside back toward the buggy, and then get inside the horses." I done the same with Don Bustamante, leaving him between his daughter-in-law and his son and ducking inside the animals. We were all four just inside the lead horses with the buggy coming along in the rear. Outside of us were the seven prisoners. I pointed toward the southeast. "We'll head that way." Chulo took the reins of the buggy horse from Wilcey and we settled down to walk over the rough prairie. I walked in the middle, sometimes looking back to see if any pursuit was developing.

If they fired they were going to have a hell of a time hitting us with all the prisoners and horses between us.

Wilcey said, "I didn't know if you wanted me to put anybody in the buggy or not. Maybe the senora."

I looked at him. He was walking just in front of me, two horses on lead. "No, goddamnit," I said. "I didn't want you to put nobody in the buggy. I'm glad you figured it out all by yourself. The buggy is intended to give us protection in case anybody feels like taking a shot at us from the back."

We walked.

Over the rough prairie. Occasionally one of the prisoners would stumble, but then they'd pick themselves up and go on. I was back near the head of the buggy horse. Linda was on my outside right. I could clearly see her head and shoulders over Chulo's horse, which was between us. She walked with that same hang-dog, face on her breast, way that she'd been ever since I'd brought her downstairs and tied her up. She looked whipped.

I don't know what it made me feel. Partly I felt sorry for her. Mostly I felt like I'd been a damn fool to have yearned for her all these years. I didn't think much of her for what she'd said to me about going back upstairs if I'd cut her bonds, but I couldn't get the thought out of my mind of what it would have felt like to have done it. Hell, it felt strange. The woman had been on my mind so many years; so many years I'd had her up on a throne, and then, by God, here she was, walking on the outside of our horse as we made a getaway from robbing a bank. Walking over the rough ground of Mexico.

How is a man supposed to feel about a woman under such a situation?

We walked. I kept looking back toward the town, but I couldn't see a single sign of pursuit developing. Sabinas Hidalgo is in a little valley, so we were mostly walking uphill.

But it is a very small, very slight valley, and, ahead, I could see the crest of the top of the valley when it would become the hot prairie again. We were heading in the general direction of Vera Cruz.

Wilcey had dropped back and was just to my front. "How do you feel, Wilcey?"

"Scared shitless," he said. He turned to look back toward the town. "I keep feeling like an entire cavalry of *Federales* is fixing to come busting out of that town and shoot the hell out of us."

"Myself," I said. "I'm just walking along here with my heart in my mouth."

From a little in front, Sam said, "Senor Wilson."

"What are you doing, Sam? You talking Mexican now so in case them *Federales* come for us you can claim you ain't one of the robbers?"

He laughed a little over that. "Sounds like a pretty good idea. But what I want to know is why we are walking? Why don't we get on the horses?"

"Well, Sam. We can only go as fast as our prisoners can walk. So it wouldn't do us much good to be mounted. And, second, you get on one of the horses and your head is going to be sticking above the crowd. Which makes for a pretty nice target in case one of them government troops takes it into his head to shoot at you."

He walked for a moment more, then said, "I never thought of that."

Wilcey said dryly, "That's why Wilson is the boss."

I turned and looked back. I figured we'd come a good three-quarters of a mile. And still there was no catch party being formed that I could see.

Outside of the circle the prisoners walked along. We were very near the top of the valley now. I looked back and it looked like the *Federales* were keeping their word.

"Stop," I said.

"What?" It was Sam, who'd moved up in front of the party.

"Stop," I said.

We came to a halt. I walked out from amongst them and looked back toward the town. It was damn near out of sight. Only the top of the cathedral was still visible. I turned back and pointed at the maid and her husband who was the manservant in the house. "You two. Go back. *Via por case. Ahora!*"

They looked uncertain and I made motions like shooting chickens. I said, *"Vamoose, vamoose!"*

They stood there like wooden Indians. "Goddamnit it," I said, "get on back home while the getting is good."

Don Bustamante spoke to them, then, and they finally began to walk off.

"Hell," Wilcey said, "you'd of thought they liked us."

"Let's make some tracks."

We made it to the crest of the little valley and started across the prairie. Now, with a little advantage in height, I could look back at the town. There was still no pursuit.

Sam asked, "What you think, Will?"

"Looking pretty good. Little too early to tell yet."

Wilcey said, "Hell, we got some distance. Let's get on these goddamn horses and cover some ground."

"Not yet," I said.

Then Linda called to me. "Senor! Senor!"

"What?"

She was stumbling badly. "Senor, please. May I ride in the carriage? I am not used to this walking and my shoes are not fit."

I didn't answer her.

"Senor? Please?"

"What?"

"Please, may I ride?"

I said, "When you remember my name."

Her husband said, "Shut your mouth, woman."

It had begun to get hot and the country was changing. Now it was all cactus and rocks and sand, with only here and there an occasional stunted tree.

Wilcey said, "Will, why the hell don't you let her ride in the buggy? She's slowing us down."

I didn't answer him, just kept slogging along. Finally, after I'd come what I guessed to be a mile from the crest of the little valley, I called another halt. I pointed at Bustamante the junior. "Go home," I said. He stood there, waiting.

I said, "No, just you. Take off walking. Now."

He looked at his wife and then back at me. I said, "Don't worry about your wife. Your father is still with us. Now start walking." I pulled out my revolver.

He said, "Senor, I am very thirsty."

"Give him a drink, Sam."

Sam handed him a canteen. He took a long pull, then poured some in his hand and washed his face off. Then he looked up at me. I could just see him over the horse that was between us. "I would like to take my wife back with me."

"No," I said. "You've had her long enough. Now it's my turn."

Wilcey said, "Will! Goddamnit!"

"Now start walking, greaser, or I'll put a bullet through

your leg and you won't be able to walk." I pulled out my revolver.

"Yes," he said. "As you say." He gave his wife one last look and then turned and started back toward town.

"Let's move," I said.

Linda said, "Please. Senor."

"Walk," I said.

We walked. The ground had got rougher. Every once in a while I looked over and watched Linda stumbling along.

When I called the next halt I didn't quite know what to do. So I said, "All right, everybody have a drink of water. Distribute them canteens, Sam."

Then I went to my saddlebags and got out a bottle of brandy and stood there sipping on that. Just standing there, leaning on my elbow against the horse's rump, thinking.

Wilcey come up and I pitched him the bottle. He took a pull and then handed it back. "Looks like we're doing pretty good," he said.

"Yeah," I said. I pushed off my horse and went outside the circle and pointed at Don Bustamante and the stable boy. "Now it's your turn," I said. "You can leave now."

Senor Bustamante said, "What about the senora? May she return with us?"

I shook my head. "Not yet."

Bustamante gave me a look. "Senor, you gave your word."

"I mean to keep it," I said. "I said if there was no trouble you would all be released unharmed. So it will be."

"You are going to leave a fragile woman alone on the prairie? Miles from her home?"

In the first place she ain't all that delicate. And I got a pretty good idea she won't have far to walk. I would imagine the *Federales* are already in pursuit. "You are to leave. Now. We are wasting time."

I took his arm and turned him and walked a few steps with him. "One other thing, senor. I don't generally say I'm sorry about robbing somebody, and I ain't. I'm a robber by trade and that's the way I make my living. But I don't ever deliberately set out to put a hardship on anyone and I know I've put a hardship on you. I don't give a damn about your son, but you've acted like a man during this time and I appreciate it. In return I'm going to try and do you a little favor." I jerked my head back toward where my party was waiting. "That man back there, Martin, your political rival, tried to hire me to assassinate you."

He looked startled for a second, glancing toward where Martin was standing, then he looked back at me and shrugged. "I am not surprised. He is an evil man."

"Well, you were lucky this time for I am not a paid killer. But there are other men who are, and he might find one. However, I believe this experience has been so bad for him that he might never attempt it again."

Bustamante nodded slowly. "It had been on my mind to ask what he was doing in my son's house."

"I had him there," I said, "on purpose. I don't like his kind of man. Not even a little bit. I used him for my purposes, and now I'm going to deal with him for your purposes."

He gave me a quick look, I shook my head. "No, I'm not going to kill him, that's not my style. However, I am going to turn him loose on the prairie in very difficult circumstances. He could possibly die, but I will not have killed him."

He studied my face, but didn't say anything.

I said, "So you are warned. If he makes it back to town he might find someone else to hire."

"I thank you, senor."

"Y'all better start walking."

He almost moved but then he didn't. He said, sort of hesitantly, "Senor, my son's wife . . ."

"She'll be fine," I said. "Don't worry."

"But would you not please release her now so that I could accompany her back?"

I gave him a flat look. "No."

"But she will come to no harm?"

"None," I said. "She will have the buggy to drive."

He still did not want to leave. Finally he said, "I take you for a man of your word."

I half grinned. "Even if I am a bank robber."

"Just so." He did not smile when he said it.

Then he waved at the stable boy. "Juan! We go!"

I started us off again. After ten minutes Wilcey said, "Say, what the hell are you up to?"

"What do you mean?"

"You've turned everyone back except the woman and that damn Martin. We've got a two-hour start. We need to be mounted and running. When the hell we going to do it?"

I stopped us. I said, "Hold up right here." There wasn't much of a circle anymore. We were just all a bunch of foot-sore wanderers leading four horses and a carriage. I walked up to Martin. Linda was off to my left, her head down, her hands folded as if they were still tied. I said, "Martin, I'm fixing to turn you loose."

Relief come all over his face. He didn't look so much like the self-important little politico he'd looked that morning. He'd undone his tie, he'd unbuttoned his vest, his black suit was all dusty and soiled, and his hair was back in his face. "*Gracias,* senor," he said. He was almost blubbering. "*Muchas gracias.* May God and the Virgin Mother bless you forever."

I said, "Martin, listen, you sorry sonofabitch. I don't reckon you ought to be bringing down God's name and

Jesus Christ's mother's name on this situation. Because you're a little greaser snake."

The relief faded and fear came over his face. "I do not understand you, senor."

I said, tight-mouthed. "You're fixing to. I need you to know one thing, you afterbirth-eating sonofabitch. You don't hire Wilson Young to kill somebody. That ain't my style. You done insulted me, you bastard, and you're going to be the one that's sorry for it. You wouldn't make a pimple on Don Bustamante's ass. I ain't going to kill you, but I hope you die." I turned and looked at the black Mexican. "Chulo. Hamstring him."

Those white teeth got big in his black face. He reached in his pocket and come out with that clasp knife of his. He came toward us, opening it as he did. "Ah," he said. "Yes, I like this."

Martin almost fainted from fear. I pulled out my revolver and stuck it in his face. I said, "You move and I will kill you."

Chulo came up, stropping that gleaming blade on his pants. He looked at me questioningly. I said, "Yes, I mean it. Hamstring the sonofabitch. I hope to hell he dies in this desert. I ain't got the heart to kill him or else I would."

Martin began to back away as Chulo approached him, but I cocked my pistol, still aimed at his head. "One more step," I said, "and I blow your fucking head off."

From behind me I heard Sam ask, "Does he mean this? Is he serious?"

And Wilcey answered him, very tight-voiced. "Yeah, he means it."

Chulo had taken Martin by the arm by then. He looked at me and I pointed down. So he took Martin and threw him on the ground. Then he looked up at me. "Which leg, senor?"

"I don't give a damn," I said. Then I said, "Wait a

minute." Linda was standing at the front of our little party looking very frightened. I said to her, "Get in the buggy."

She just stared back at me. I turned. "Sam, put her in the buggy. Now."

I watched while he went to her, took her by both arms, escorted her to the carriage, and helped her into the seat.

Chulo still had Martin down, Martin's face in the dust, holding one arm behind his back. Martin was not saying much, but I could hear his breathing from where I stood, ten feet away.

Wilcey said, "You sure you want to do this, Will?"

"Yes," I said.

"You know he'll never be able to walk back. You might as well shoot him in the head."

I turned on him. "Listen, Wilcey," I said, "you are always coming at me with that better-than-me shit. Did he try to hire you to gun down somebody?"

He didn't answer.

I said, "Well? Did he?"

He looked away. "You know goddamn good and well he didn't."

"Did he pay you the insult of treating you like a hired killer?"

He still wouldn't look at me.

"Did he?"

"No," he finally said.

"How the hell would that have made you feel if he had?"

He turned away. He said, "Goddamnit, do what you have to do."

"Oh, yeah. So long as you ain't involved."

I looked over at Chulo who was waiting expectantly. When you hamstring a man you cut the tendon in the back of his thigh. You might as well have broken his leg because he ain't going to be able to walk on it.

I studied on it for a long moment. But the one thing that kept coming back to my mind was the little sonofabitch trying to hire me to kill a good man like Don Bustamante. I said to Chulo, "Cut him!"

He grinned at me, flicked the edge of the shining blade with his thumb, then made a quick slash. Martin screamed. I could see the blood immediately running out of the cut in his pants. He was hamstringed. Good and proper. I said, loudly, "All right. Now we go. Mount up. Sam, you're driving the buggy."

We left Martin laying there on the prairie, cursing and crying and bleeding. He'd probably die before help came. Hell, I didn't give a damn. Man like Martin should be killed. And I believed that as much as I believed anything.

I looked back at the buggy. Sam had gotten in and was driving it. Linda was sitting beside him, leaned back in the seat, her head back, her eyes closed. We had all mounted up and Sam had tied his horse on behind.

"Let's move," I said.

As we rode I looked back. Far off in the distance I could just see a sign of movement as Don Bustamante and the sable boy headed back for town. There was still no pursuit that I could see.

We had the horses in a slow lope. The time had come now to get as much distance as possible. Those *Federales* would be coming and there was no mistake to that.

As we rode I tried to see a map in my head. I had changed my mind about Vera Cruz. It was too far. But we could reach Tampico in three days of hard riding from where we were.

I did not expect the *Federales* from Sabinas to be able to overtake us. We had too big of a lead for that. But along the route we were taking, Monterey and Saltillo and Ciudad Victoria lay just to our west, and Reynosa was just to the east. And all of these towns had detachments of *Federales* and all of them had telegraph offices.

Which meant that we could be intercepted along the way. The only thing they didn't know was where we were headed and they could just as well imagine, as not, that we had taken a southeasterly direction in order to throw them off the scent and would later change it once we were out of sight.

We rode hard for an hour. There was no chance to talk as fast as we were going, but Wilcey kept throwing little glances back at me. Over the flat prairie the buggy was having no trouble keeping up. I looked back at Linda several times, but she had not changed. She still sat there, leaned back, her hands folded in her lap, her eyes closed.

I wondered what she must be thinking or what she felt was in store for her.

But then I didn't even know the answer to that myself for I hadn't made my mind up.

Finally I called a halt. I had not meant to make it a full stop, just to get down and walk the horses and let them rest. But Sam called to me. "She wants to see you."

I walked back to the buggy. She didn't raise her head and she didn't open her eyes. She said, "Senor, *por favor*, what are you going to do with me?"

I said, "I don't know. I haven't decided yet."

She said, "Please, senor, I am so hungry and so tired."

I walked over to Wilcey's horse and opened his saddle-bag. He was carrying the grub. We still had some cold meat, and I cut off a chunk and took it back to her. "Here," I said, "eat this. Sam, hand her the canteen."

She roused enough to take the piece of beef in her hands, but she just looked at it. I imagine to her eyes it looked a little the worse for wear, but it was still food. I said, "You get hungry enough, you'll eat it."

Chulo and Wilcey were sitting on the ground holding their horses' reins in their hands. I got the bottle of brandy out of my saddlebags and sat down beside them. I took a drink and then passed it around. They drank and didn't say anything. Finally Wilcey wiped his mouth and looked over at me. He said, "Will, what the hell are you playing at?"

I said, carefully, "I don't know what you mean."

"Yeah, you do. You're fixing to get all our asses killed. You're dragging that goddamn girl around with you and you know we ought to be making tracks and heading for Vera Cruz just as fast as we can."

I said, "We ain't going to Vera Cruz."

He looked at me. "Oh, yeh? Where we going?"

"Tampico," I said. I was smoking a cigarillo and I dropped it between my boots and ground it out with my boot.

"When you decide that?"

"About an hour ago," I said. "Or maybe sooner. I hadn't really given it much thought."

"Why?"

I got up. "Tampico's closer. I don't think we can make Vera Cruz."

He said, "Well, I sure appreciate you telling us." He took the bottle of brandy from where it was laying on the ground and had a drink. Then he said, "But you ain't told me what you're going to do with that goddamn woman."

I had walked a few steps away. Now I turned back to face him. With a little heat in my voice, I said, "Listen, Wilcey, you better let this alone. This goes back a long ways, and I ain't going to talk to you about it. It ain't none of your goddamn business."

"Ain't none of my goddamn business!" He got up and took a step toward me. "Are you crazy? Here's me and Chulo and Sam. You're putting our goddamn asses in a bind because of that damn girl. Don't you tell me it ain't any of my goddamn business!"

He was hot and no mistake. I said, "You goddamn well better shut up. In fact you had better get on that horse because we're fixing to pull out." I turned to my animal and mounted up. "Now get in the saddle," I told him, "if you're going with me."

He stood there staring at me. I said, "Listen, ain't no law says you got to go with me. You can take your share of the money and go off in any direction you want to."

He looked at me for another half a second and then got on his horse.

I said, "Let's go."

I looked back and Sam was slapping the buggy horse with the reins. Linda was still holding the piece of meat in her hands, her head leaned back. She didn't look as if she'd tried to eat. Well, that was her affair.

I put us into a lope and held it over the rough, flat land. By now I wasn't so concerned about pursuit from behind as I was somebody waylaying us from Monterey and Reynosa or even, though it seemed a little far, Ciudad Victoria.

It had now come afternoon and it had become hot out there on the prairie. I kept us moving at a good clip. I imagined that, by now, about half of Mexico was looking for us. You don't commit a robbery the way we'd done, doing kidnapping and holding prisoners, without making the law get kind of angry at you.

The next time I called a halt I could see Wilcey was ready to get into it. I'd sat down on the ground and was eating a little meat and tortillas and drinking some brandy. He and Chulo came over. He said, sounding angry, "Now what are you going to do about that goddamn girl?"

I said, "Wilcey, you better quit bringing this up. I don't

want trouble with you. But you're starting to get me just a little hot."

He took his hat off and wiped his brow with his sleeve. Then he hunkered down, facing me. He said, "Well, you got to decide to do something. Dragging her along in that buggy is slowing us down. And if we get in a gunfight I doubt she can pull her weight. I figure you owe us more than to do us this way."

Well, he had a point. I got up and walked a few feet away and stood there staring at the horizon. On the one hand I didn't want to be unfair to my partners, but I found myself totally—and I mean all there was—unable to turn loose of the woman. Why I'd been damn fool enough to let her get hold of my mind and heart the way I had was beyond me.

But there it was and I didn't know what to do about it. I turned and walked back. I said, "Wilcey, you act like an old woman about half the time. I ain't going to go on what you say." I looked at Chulo. "Nigger, tell me what you think?"

There was trouble in his face. He didn't put them big white teeth in his black face and say, *"No hay de que."* It doesn't matter. Instead he looked down at the ground and said, "Well, I think it is not so good that we are going so slowly. I thenk the woman is perhaps slowing us up." Then he said, quickly, "But you are the *jefe*. And I will do as you say. You have always taken care of matters before."

Wilcey suddenly jerked off his hat and slammed it against his thigh in disgust. He turned on Chulo. "Goddamnit, that ain't the way you talked about it to me. You told me you was going to tell him to get rid of that damn woman. What are you doing, backing off?"

Chulo looked miserable. He said, "Well, it is not so easy to say thes to an hombre that has been your partner for these years." He wouldn't look at Wilcey.

"Ah, shit!" Wilcey said. He put his hat back on and

looked at me. "Well, if he won't say it, I will. Ain't none of us likes it. Now, goddamnit, I put up with you getting our asses in a bind robbing that bank in Sabinas so you could see her. Well, you've seen her. All right. We got away with it. Mostly. And I ain't holding it against you. But now it's time to make some tracks and get away. We got the money and you know, better'n any man I reckon is alive today, how to get us out of here and get us to a place where we can spend this money. I mean—" He stopped. Then he said, looking a little embarrassed, "I mean, goddamn, we're your partners."

I kind of flinched at that. I got up from where I was hunkered down. I said, "Yeah, I know." I walked a few feet away, thinking. Hell, I knew I was doing them wrong. But I didn't know what to do about Linda. I turned and walked back. "Look," I said, "let's leave this alone for the time being. I'll decide tonight. I don't know what else to tell you."

Wilcey looked amazed. "You mean you're going to keep her around the rest of the afternoon?"

I said, steadily, "Yes. And I don't want to hear no more about it."

"Ah, shit," he said, and slapped his thigh again.

"Let it alone, Wilcey," I said. "Goddamnit, this ain't easy for me. Now let's mount up and get on down the road toward Tampico."

We done it, Wilcey cussing under his breath. Just mumbling loud enough so that I could hear him. I didn't pay him no mind. Behind us Sam looked content driving the buggy. Linda looked like she'd passed out.

Well, wasn't nothing I could do about that.

Just after we pulled out, Wilcey put his horse up next to mine. He said, "Will, get rid of her right now. Just give her the reins to that buggy and point her toward home. We could make Tampico by tomorrow night if we rode hard. We get there we got plenty of money to buy all the women you need."

I just looked at him. I said, "No. Now let's get this show on down the road."

I pushed us hard the rest of the afternoon. Whenever we stopped to rest the horses Wilcey would look at me, but he wouldn't say anything. Finally it come night. I took us another hour and then called a halt. There wasn't no natural cover on the bald ass prairie so I just said, "Whoa! Here's where we stop."

We got the horses unsaddled and put them on short picket, got our bedrolls laid down, and got ready to settle in. It was going to be a cold camp. I had no intentions of having a fire built that would be a beacon to any *Federales* that was wandering around. Linda had got out of the buggy and was just standing there. I went up to her. I said, "Well, you want something to eat? I seen you didn't eat the beef I gave you. Sorry, princess, but that's all we got. So you either eat that or go hungry."

She didn't say anything, just stood there, her head hung down. I wanted to take her by the shoulders and give her a good shaking, but all I did was say, "Well, I reckon you will make your bed on the seat of the buggy. I'll get you a blanket."

I went and tore into my bedroll and come back with my blanket. "Here," I said, shoving it into her hands. "I reckon you can handle it from here." I turned and walked to where my partners was grouped up. They were sitting drinking brandy. Chulo was eating tortillas and Sam was smoking. None of them would look at me directly. I sat down and took the brandy bottle from Wilcey and had a pull. I said, "We're only going to rest about four hours. Then we're going to make some more tracks."

Wilcey said, "Yeah, let's hurry. We're having a hard time keeping up with that buggy."

I gave him a glance, but didn't say anything.

Sam said, "Will, I want to ask you something."

"Go ahead."

He held up his hand. "Now understand, I ain't gettin' uppity about this. I know I'm the new man on the job."

"I said go ahead."

He said, "Well, I'm just wondering what you're going to do with that girl if the *Federales* jump us. Seems to me that that would give you a little more to do than if she wasn't here."

I looked at Wilcey. He said, "I haven't been talking to Sam. But a goddamn fool could see the danger she's giving us all."

Sam said, "Will, I may be talking out of school, but I don't see what you're going to do with the woman. She's pretty as hell and no question. But you ain't even taken her behind the bushes and fucked her. You know you can't take her into Tampico with us. She'd scream first thing and we'd have every lawman in Mexico after us. I'm just trying to get what you're after with her. I imagine you got a good reason."

Wilcey said, that little dry tone in his voice, "Don't bet on it."

I ignored Wilcey and told Sam, "Right now I don't know. You just got to trust me."

Wilcey said, "Shit!"

But Sam said, "Well, I reckon I ain't got much choice. You are the boss and you plenty good by us so far."

Wilcey said, "And speaking of that woman. I believe she's leaving us."

I looked over my shoulder. She'd walked away from the buggy about fifty yards. She looked as if she was heading for a clump of mesquite. I said, "I got an idea where she's going."

Wilcey said, goading me, "You mean even them beautiful senoritas have to take a piss once in a while?"

I looked up at the sky. The sun was just starting to dip into the horizon. It would be dark in another half hour. I said, "Sam, you take the first watch. About an hour. Then Chulo, then Wilcey, and then me. As soon as everybody gets something to eat we better sack out and get as much rest as possible. We're going to really move tomorrow."

My main worry was the terrain. Out on the bald ass prairie as we were there was no natural protection. If we'd get jumped there'd be no place to fort up and we'd probably end up in a running gun fight. I knew my partners could see the same thing so that's what I figured was making them so jumpy about the girl. Well, all I could figure was, if we did get bushwhacked, I'd just cut her loose in the buggy and make a run for it.

I saw her coming back from the bushes. I'd never been too worried she'd take off. Hell, where was she going to go?

She climbed into the seat and I picked up a canteen and carried it over to her. "You want some water?"

She was laying on her side, her eyes closed. They fluttered open as I spoke. She looked very tired. She also looked as if she'd been crying. She slowly straightened up and took the canteen from my hand. I'd unscrewed the cap so she tilted it up and drank just a little. I asked her, "You want some brandy?"

She just shook her head no.

I said, "Might make you feel better."

She said, "No, thank you, senor."

"Suit yourself," I said. I turned, but she called my name. "Senor, Wilson Young."

I turned back to her. "Finally remember my name?"

"Senor, what are you going to do with me? Are you going to hurt me or kill me?"

"I don't kill women," I said. "And I try not to hurt them.

If you mean am I going to beat you up, the answer is no."

"Are you going to leave me on the prairie alone?"

"No," I said. I studied her for a moment. You could see the ravages of her ordeal on her face. She didn't look quite so pretty. I said, "I don't know why I'm keeping you. But it's too late to turn you loose now. Perhaps when we get near a town I'll take you to the outskirts so you can get help and get back home. But you might as well go to sleep now. Obviously I'm not going to do anything with you tonight."

She said, "I am very much afraid."

"I guess I would be in your shoes, too."

She dropped her eyes slightly and asked, almost in a whisper, "Why are you doing this to me?"

Well, I didn't quite know how to answer that one because I didn't know why I was doing it either. I just said, "You go to sleep. And don't worry. You're going to be all right."

It had come dusk, and instead of going back to my partners, I walked off a little ways out on the prairie and stood there smoking. Hell, the woman hadn't done anything to me. What I'd felt I'd felt, I'd done to myself. All I had against her was that I couldn't have her.

But I still couldn't make myself let her go.

I flipped my cigarillo away and turned and walked back to where my bedroll lay. Everyone except Sam had turned in. He was sitting, smoking, his rifle in his hand.

"Well, Sam," I said, "we made a good payday today."

He shrugged. "Money ain't no good unless you can spend it."

I took off my boots and got into my bedroll. It was turning off a little cool. "We'll be doing that soon enough. Keep an eye on the woman."

"Yeah," he said.

I put my hat over my face. "I hope we strike water early tomorrow. These horses are going to need it pretty soon."

EIGHT

We got away an hour or so after midnight, judging by the moon. Linda woke up as Sam was hitching up the horse, but she didn't say anything. I imagine she'd spent nights that was a good deal more comfortable than she'd just had on a buggy seat.

I took it pretty easy on the horses, striking a slow pace. They'd been good watered before we'd left, but I figured they was starting to get plenty thirsty. I knew there were any number of little streams cutting the prairie and I knew we'd get to one before too much longer, but I didn't want to take a chance of weakening the animals by working them too hard when they needed water.

We just kept a steady walk, just getting on over the prairie. I stopped us twice before it come dawn, but nobody had much to say. By now we were getting low on grub, and most of the meat having gone bad. There were still plenty of tortillas and we made do with those as best we could, though Linda wouldn't take any.

Then, just as it come good light, I saw the tops of little line of trees away off in the distance, maybe a mile, mile and a half away. I pointed and said, "There's water. I believe, if I remember the map correctly that it would be Cibolo creek, which, the last time I saw it, was a pretty little stream."

Wilcey said, "Why don't you ask your girlfriend?"

I ignored that and let my horse drop back until I was riding next to the buggy. "Is that Cibolo creek, Sam?"

He nodded. "It would just about have to be. It be the first one we've come to since we headed south."

I rode back up to the front of the party. Wilcey said, "Do you know where we are?"

"Pretty close," I said. "I figure we're about due east of Monterey. That creek goes through it. And if that be the case that's put us about seventy, seventy-five miles from Tampico. We make some good time today and we could be mighty close by tomorrow night."

Now we could see the line of trees easily. It meandered over the prairie, following the course of the creek, and generally headed due west toward Monterey. To our east, toward the coast, the land fell away. But it rose toward Monterey, which made me feel a little uneasy. A catch party coming out of Monterey would be able to see us easily and from a good distance away. We stuck out, I felt sure, out on that bald ass prairie, like a fly in the butter dish. It made me anxious to get on past Monterey.

But then that didn't make any sense for Ciudad Victoria was just another fifteen or twenty miles further south and just west of the line we were taking. I thought of turning due east toward the coast and heading south from there, but there'd be towns along that route, too, and just as many *Federales*. No, we were better off threading the distance between them and waiting until we were nearly to Tampico before turning for the coast.

The horses had begun to smell the water and they were moving faster with no urging. We were sweeping up to the banks of the creek, having to hold our horses back to keep them from plunging into the water.

I dismounted and said, "All right, loosen the cinches and take the bits out of their mouths so they can graze. We're going to take a little rest here."

I loosened my horse's saddle cinch and then led him down to the creek. He plunged his head into the water almost to his eyes. He was that thirsty. I let him drink a little, then pulled him back and tied him to a low branch. A hot, tired horse will founder himself on water if you'll let him. He went to grazing and I sat down and lit a cigarillo. Sam had pulled the buggy in under the trees and he was busy unhitching the horse while Chulo and Wilcey were watering theirs. Linda got slowly down from the buggy seat and walked stiffly down to the creek. I'd imagine that a woman used to all the comforts of life could get pretty stove up sitting in a buggy seat for near two days. While I watched, she took a handkerchief out of her sleeve and wet it in the creek and began dabbing at her face with it. She was starting to look a little dusty and travel worn.

It was a pretty little creek, about ten feet across, maybe two feet deep at the most, and lined with willows and mesquite and some low bushes of a type I didn't know. The banks were about two feet high which made it a fair to average place to fort up if a man had to. Its worst drawback was that a determined band of horsemen could get inside the banks and come charging right straight down the creek, and if you didn't kill or discourage them fast enough, they'd be right in amongst you.

I got up and found a few pieces of wood and began building a fire, building it under the biggest of the willows which would perhaps hide most of the smoke.

Wilcey came up, watching. He handed me the bottle of brandy and I had a pull. He said, "Is that wise, building that fire?"

"Well, no, not really. But the wood is mesquite and won't smoke too much and we're in under these trees so that ought to help. But I figure we need to heat up some of this meat where we might can get it down. It's getting a little rank and we need to eat. Maybe if we burn the hell out of it, it'll be edible."

He said, "Hell, I ain't had no trouble with it. And I seen you eating some and Chulo and Sam."

I knew what he was getting at, but I just let it lay. Hell, he had a point and no mistake. So he was entitled to at least do a little complaining.

Sam finished with the buggy horse, tied him near the buggy, and then went for his own. Linda came up from the creek, dabbing her face with the wet handkerchief. She hesitated as she walked by the little fire I was building, and for a moment, I thought she was going to stop. But she went up and sat on the ground in front of a tree and rested her back up against the trunk.

I had the fire going and I went over and got a piece of meat out of my saddlebag. It was wrapped in an old rag and looked pretty bad. We'd had it with us about five or six days, and what with the heat and all, it wasn't none the better for the wear. But I took out my knife and cut off some of the outside and then cut me a green mesquite switch and stuck it on the end of that. My partners were hunkered around the campfire drinking rum and water out of their tin cups.

"It's getting serious, Will," Wilcey said. "We're getting low on whiskey."

Chulo said, "An' this is no *bueno por nada!* When you are running out of wheeskey, it is a serious time to hurry."

I was toasting the beef over the little fire. "What we got left?"

"Two bottles of rum and one of the brandy, but it ain't quite full."

I said, dryly, "Well, we'll just have to rough it out."

When I thought the meat was burned enough to kind of kill some of the taste, I taken my cup, poured a little rum in it, added enough water to make it too weak for a man, but just about right for a highborn senorita, and then walked over to where she was sitting on the ground. I held the stick with the meat on it out to her and the cup of rum and water. "Here," I said, "you got to eat some of this."

She thought she was going to say no, but then she got a little whiff of the meat, which was looking some better. She hesitated. I said, "Look, you got to eat. You ain't eaten in a good while and if I turn you loose you're going to have to have enough strength to get to safety."

She took the stick and I handed her the cup of rum, then I sat down beside her. She still hesitated, like she didn't know how to eat meat on a stick. I said, "Quit worrying about whether you're going to look like the grand lady or not and start gnawing. We ain't got no doilies or silver plates out here."

Well, she finally commenced eating. She started slowly at first, just taking little nibbling bites, but pretty soon was getting after it with good pace. I guess even ladies have appetites, too.

I got out a cigarillo and lit it and watched her. She took a few sips out of the rum and water, made a face each time, but kept on drinking.

I sat there not real sure what to say. Seemed like I should say something but I couldn't think of anything. She sure looked whipped down. She'd gotten some grease off the beef on her face and she kept wiping at it with the back of her wrist, but all she was doing was smearing it. It seemed kind of hard to believe that this woman could have so run my head and my heart. Hell, I'd been with her better than a day and I'd never so much as laid a hand on her. And it hadn't been because I was such a gentleman; it was because I just didn't feel no big urge. I suddenly asked her, "How come you never had no kid?"

She looked at me, but didn't say anything. Just went on eating.

I said, "You and your husband. You was married plenty long. You're Catholic, I know. How come you never had no children?"

She finally said, "Please, senor, I know very little about these kind of things."

"Oh hell," I said, "you're a woman, ain't you? How can you not know about such things?"

I suddenly felt a great desire to shock her, to get her attention, to talk a little rough to her. I said, "Maybe you and that little husband of yours never did anything. Eh?"

She looked away.

"Well, did you? Do you know how?"

She kept her face away from me. She'd stopped chewing on the beef. I said, "Ah, the hell with you." I got up and walked over to where Sam was sitting on the side of the bank. "Here," I said, "give me a drink of that rum."

He handed me the bottle and I had a long pull, the fiery stuff burning all the way down, but then spreading and warming up my innards. I squatted down beside him. "She ever talk much, Sam?" I jerked my head back toward Linda.

"Naw," he said. "I tried a little just to pass the time, but she don't say much of anything. Just lay over in the corner of the seat and look like she's going to cry. About the only thing she ever say was to ask when you were going to turn her loose."

"She call me by name?"

He shook his head. "No. She just call you *el jefe*. Except sometimes she called you the bandit chief."

I said, "Hmm." If I'd had dreams about this they were rapidly going up in smoke.

Sam looked at me curiously. "You know I reckon I know as much as I'm supposed to know about you and that girl. And that's next to nothing."

I said, "It don't matter. I'll tell you someday. Right now you know enough from Wilcey to know I'm acting like a goddamn fool." I stood up and walked over to my horse to move him to a little better grazing. Wilcey come up. He said. "Will, we are wasting an awful lot of time here. Don't you reckon we better get moving."

"In a little while," I said. "These horses need the rest."

He glanced over to where Linda was sitting in the shade of the tree. Then he looked back at me and said, with an edge in his voice, "The horses or that goddamn girl?"

I was about to get enough of it. I'd let him mouth off and mouth off, figuring he had a certain right, but he was about to go too far. "You shut up, Wilcey. Understand?"

But he wouldn't back off. He said, "No, my God, I don't understand!" He flung his arms out toward Chulo and Sam and said, "And there's two others over there don't by God understand neither. Chulo has said he's never seen you play the fool before, and Sam can't believe it's you, Wilson Young. And neither can I! You are making a goddamn fool out of yourself over that goddamn girl, and you ain't acting nothing like the Wilson Young I threw my gear in with."

"Now listen, Wilcey—"

"No, goddamnit, you listen! I been listening ever since you come up with this hare-brained idea of robbing that bank. All right, you done it. You made it work when I didn't believe it could. But now we're out of it. Now we got a chance to get away. Why in hell are you putting us in danger over some woman?"

"This is a goddamn dangerous business as you have known from the first! I never misled you about that."

"No! And I never complained before. Because I never seen you take undue risks like this before. Sure, we got into plenty of danger, but I never before seen you get us into any for no good reason."

I had never seen him so worked up in the three or four years he'd been my partner. And he'd never challenged me so strongly as he was doing now. Over his shoulder I could see that Sam and Chulo had stood up. They were trying to act as if they weren't watching or listening, but I could see them, every now and again, shoot a glance our way.

Wilcey said, intently, "Listen, just tell me what you're going to do with her. Just tell me something I can understand. Something that makes sense. If you can tell me something that I can understand, something that makes the risk worthwhile, why then I'll quit worrying. But what are you going to do with her— Take her to Tampico and marry her? Take her to Texas and set up housekeeping? Keep her in a hotel room for a week and fuck her brains out and then kill her?" He was looking at me intently. "What? Goddamnit, what are you going to do with her!"

Of course I had nothing to tell him. I just had to stand there feeling bad because I knew I was doing wrong by my partners. Could I say to him, to all of them, that I couldn't let her go because I wanted to keep her with me as long as possible. Hoping, I guess, that something would happen. I am sure to God didn't know what? What could happen? Her suddenly call me to her side and say she'd been mistaken, that she should have waited for me, and now she'd go with me anywhere? Hell, the woman hadn't even remembered me. What else did I expect? Her to beg forgiveness for the wrong she'd done me? What wrong?

So I had no answers other than I couldn't bear to part with her before it was absolutely necessary. Which was pretty goddamn dumb.

Wilcey said, "Well, you going to answer me?"

I looked over at the girl. She was watching and listening. I said, "Wilcey, I don't have anything to tell you. If you and Chulo and Sam want to take your share and go on, I will understand and will have no complaints."

"Aw, shit!" he said. He stepped back and looked at me, shaking his head. "You can say that, can't you? Knowing goddamn good and well that we have plain and simple got used to you running the show. Oh, fine, we could probably stumble along by ourselves. But we gonna do a hell of a lot better with you calling the shots." He shook his head. "No, Will, that old dog won't hunt. Somebody's leaving, all right, but it ain't us." He jerked his head out from his side toward Linda and said, "It's her is going to leave."

I said, "Now, Wilcey, I want you to leave this alone."

"I'm not going to," he said. He glanced back. Chulo and Sam had walked a few steps toward us. He looked back at me. "It don't make no difference about them. I'm doing this on my own. But that girl is going to go and now."

"No, she's not," I told him. "I'm not about to turn her loose in the middle of the prairie."

"Listen," he said, "wasn't no more than a few hours ago you told me this creek runs right on into Monterey and that we ain't no more than a few miles from there." He pointed up the creek. "All you got to do is turn her loose in that buggy and let her follow this creek and she'll be in Monterey within two hours. Now she's rested and she's eat and that buggy horse is rested. Ain't nothing to keep her from making it."

Well, I didn't know what to say. If all I was worried about was turning her loose on the prairie, then I didn't have a leg to stand on for he was exactly right that there'd be little danger her following the creek to Monterey. So I just said, "No."

He leaned toward me, cocking his head, good and angry now. "What do you mean no! How the hell can you say no? Listen, Wilson, what the hell you got in—"

I started to turn away. There was nothing I could say. But I wasn't going to let her go. Wilcey suddenly reached out and grabbed me by the shoulder and spun me back around. Instinctively my hand went down for my gun, but I stopped. "Don't you ever do that again," I said. "Don't you ever!"

He looked at my hand where it had dropped down toward my gun. Then he looked up at my face. I moved my hand away and took a deep breath. He just shook his head. "No, you won't kill me. I ain't worried about that. That ain't your style, to kill a partner. If you was ever going to kill me, you'd of done it in that line camp when we was both going out of our heads."

I said, "It's time for us to mount up. We got to get moving."

"No," he said.

I looked at him in surprise. He'd been the one so anxious to get going.

"No," he said again. "We're going to get that girl settled right here and now. You're going to get her off your mind once and for all because until you do you ain't worth a damn either to yourself or to any of us."

"You're kind of taking a little something on yourself, ain't you?"

"You damn right I am, because it's clear you can't think straight." He looked at me a long moment, kind of drawing himself up. He appeared to be about to say something he wasn't dead sure about. Finally he said, "Either one of two things is going to happen!"

I said, "And what would those be, Wilcey?"

"Well, goddamnit, either you're going to take that woman behind them bushes and fuck her and get it out of your head that she's any different from any other. Or—"

He stopped.

I looked at him, a little startled. But I said, "Or what?"

He said quietly, "Or I'm going to get her out of your head by going over there and putting a bullet right between her eyes."

We stood there staring at each other.

After a long second he said, "Make no mistake I will."

"Have you lost your mind, Wilcey?"

He said, just a touch unsteadily, "No. Now you make up your mind. Which is it going to be? You going to go find out her legs open just like any other woman's or do I shoot her?"

I was that amazed I couldn't speak for a moment. I knew Wilcey had always been bitter at women ever since his wife had left him, so bitter that he'd never taken up with any but whores, even when we'd first got to California and we weren't wanted men. But I didn't think he could be bitter enough to just up and shoot a woman.

He said, "Well? Which is it going to be? Either take her down the creek to some of the bushes. We got time for that because it's going to get you back to being Wilson Young. Or—"

I just shook my head. "Get your horse cinched up, Wilcey. We're pulling out."

"I mean it," he said. He took two steps in Linda's direction and stopped, looking back at me.

"Stay away from her, Wilcey. This joke is going too far."

"It's no joke," he said. "I got to do something to bring you to your senses before you get us all killed."

He took another step and I pulled my revolver and leveled it down on him. To my memory it was the first time I'd ever leveled down on a partner since I'd threatened Tod Richter in the so long ago. He stopped, watching me. "You won't shoot me," he said. "I already know that. It wouldn't be your style to kill a partner."

I cocked my revolver. Out of the corner of my eye I could see Chulo and Sam staring at us. Linda had arisen from where she'd been sitting against the tree. I wondered if she spoke enough English to know what was going on.

Wilcey said again, "You won't kill me."

"No," I said, "I won't. But you take one more step toward her and I'll damn well shoot you in the leg."

"What, and leave me here for the *Federales* to hang? Naw, you wouldn't do that either. That'd be the same as killing me."

"I won't leave you here. I'll sling you in the back of that buggy. You won't die, but you won't feel so good either."

He stared at me a long moment trying, I reckoned, to decide if I meant it. Finally he said, "Aw, shit, Will! Goddamnit, I was only doing what I thought would help."

I know," I said. I uncocked my revolver and put it back in the holster.

He said, "I was just trying to get you back to being Wilson Young."

"I know it."

"That goddamn woman has had you acting like you've taken leave of your senses."

I said, "I know it."

"Aw, shit!" he said.

I turned to Chulo and Sam. "Let's get mounted up and

move out. Sam, get your buggy hitched. Wilcey, be sure the canteens are full."

While we were getting ready to pull out, Wilcey come up to me. He, like all of us, was looking tired and some drawed taut. He rubbed his beard stubble and said, "Will, I'm sorry about that."

"Don't think nothing about it," I said. I pulled my saddle cinch tight and reached up and slipped the bits in my horse's mouth.

He said, "I was bluffing. I'd of never shot that girl."

"I knew that," I said. "But it made me think, Wilcey. And I ought to get this sorted out in my mind in the next couple of hours and then I'll do something about her."

He started to turn away and then stopped. "But were you bluffing about shooting me in the leg?"

I gave him the barest of smiles as I mounted up. "We'll never know now, will we? Let's move out."

We splashed across the creek and moved through the trees, Sam having to detour a little to find a place where the trees were wide enough apart for the buggy to go through.

Then we were back on the prairie. It was near noon by now and the sun was high and, after shading up under the trees, seemed hotter than ever.

With the horses rested I set us at a pretty good clip, walking them for half an hour and then putting them in a trot for a like amount of time.

The prairie stayed clear. Somehow, coming back out in the open as we were, after being somewhat protected by the creek, I felt more apprehensive. It just kept hitting me over and over what easy targets we'd be out there, especially if we were attacked by any size of a force.

Hell, I suddenly thought, I got to get rid of this girl. In fact, it really began to hit me how foolish I'd been in dragging her this far. I, all of a sudden, began to feel a real urgency to get shut of her. Wilcey was riding just in front of me and I come up abreast of him and then pulled us all down to a walk. I looked back, calculating. The line of trees had fallen out of sight below the horizon, but I calculated it couldn't be much more than four or five miles back. I could send her quartering off to hit it and then follow it all the way into Monterey, or I could wait until we got abreast of Ciudad Victoria and send her that way. There was, if I remembered correctly, a road that run southwest out of Matamoros on into Ciudad Victoria. If that wasn't too much further, I could send her that way and she'd make it easy.

I said to Wilcey, "I'm going to get shut of her."

"When?"

"Quick's I can." I called across to Chulo, "Hey, Nigger, how far you reckon to the Matamoros, Ciudad Victoria road?"

He looked around, pushing back his sombrero and rubbing his chin as he studied the terrain. Finally he shrugged, *"Yo no se."* I don't know. "Perhaps not far. Perhaps further."

"Ahhh, you dumb *Meskin*," I said in disgust. He didn't have no idea. I reached back in my saddlebag and got out a bottle of rum and took a drink, then passed it to Wilcey. He had a pull while I uncapped my canteen and drank enough to kill the burning taste of the rum.

I thought a minute more and then capped my canteen and looked up at the sky. "I'll know in an hour," I said. "If we don't hit that road by then I'll just point her west and wish her good luck."

Wilcey gave me that wry grin of his but didn't say anything.

We kept on. After a little we passed some old adobe ruins where another Mexican farmer hadn't been able to make it on the dry prairie. Then we passed a little creek that was almost dry. The condition of the creek was as good evidence as any why the farmer hadn't made it. But it did have banks, shallow as they were, and a few stunted trees still lined its course, enough to make me note it in my mind as cover if we were jumped.

I dropped back and rode along by the buggy. Linda had wet her handkerchief from Sam's canteen and had it pressed to her face. She seemed to be feeling a little better since she'd had a rest and got some food down. She looked up as I pulled my horse alongside, but there was nothing in her face. I said, "I'm sending you home soon."

"Yes? When?"

"As soon as we hit the road to Ciudad Victoria. I'm going to turn you loose then. You'll have the buggy. It's easy to drive. I'm sure you've driven one before."

"Oh, yes," she said quickly. A little life came into her face.

"It will only be a few miles into Ciudad Victoria, and I'm sure you'll be safe there. I'll give you some money in case you should need it."

"Oh, no," she said. "That won't be necessary. I have people there, kinfolk."

I shrugged. "It was your husband's money anyway."

At that she dropped her head.

I rode a moment more trying to think of something to say for what had happened. I didn't have the words for it because I didn't understand it myself. It was, I guess, as Wilcey had said, I'd lost my head over the woman and had quit being Wilson Young. She probably wasn't a bad woman, but in just the little time I'd come to know her, she sure didn't strike me as a woman worth going crazy over. Probably she and Bustamante the junior were a pretty good match. I know they didn't either one seem worth throwing your gear and luck in with.

Finally I just said, "I'm sorry for what I've done to you Mrs. Bustamante. And I hope you get out of this all right."

Just then I heard Wilcey sing out. He yelled, "Will, we got company coming and it goddamn sure looks like trouble."

I stood up in my stirrups and shaded my eyes, trying to see as far ahead as possible. They were coming over a rise to the southwest. There were a good number, a dozen or more, but at the distance, maybe two miles, I couldn't get a good count. But I didn't have to worry about whether they was going to be friendly or not. Wasn't no outfit of horsemen running around Mexico of that size going to be anything but law or bandits.

Just then Chulo yelled. "*Federales.* For sure!"

I turned to Sam. Linda was staring up in the buggy, shading her eyes. Now she turned to me, her eyes glittering, her lips pulled back over her sharp-looking teeth. She said, "Now you will be punished!"

But I didn't pay her no mind. I said to Sam, "turn this buggy around and don't waste no time getting back to those adobe walls we passed. Get them horses in a safe place. We lose one of them we're up shit creek!"

Linda said, "You must turn me loose! You said!"

I looked at her. "Lady, you're the last hostage we got. I never thought you'd come in handy, but even you will do now. Jerk her down on the seat, Sam, and hang on to her. Now git!"

He wheeled the buggy, whipping up the horse, while I rode forward to Wilcey and Chulo. They were standing up in their stirrups. The troops had obviously seen us now for they were putting their horses forward at a good canter. "It's *Federales* all right," Wilcey said grimly. "Well, we're in for it now."

"Let's start falling back," I said. "That little dry creek is about a half mile back, but we're really going to head for them adobe walls."

Wilcey said, "Will, why don't we run for it. Sam ain't too far away to mount up."

I just said, "Which way you want to run, Wilcey? We got them coming from the front and they's bound to be some coming from the back. And I wouldn't doubt there's a bunch out of Monterey coming from the side. Now let's fall back. But not too fast."

We turned and put our horses in a slow lope. I looked back every once in a while. I wanted them to do a little catching up. When we were about a quarter of a mile from the little creek I told them, "Now you two hit it. Go on past that little creek aways so they'll think you're heading for those adobe walls. Raise all the dust you can. I sent Sam heading for there and they'll see his dust. I want them all to think we're heading that way. Then after you're a little ways past, walk your horses back. Ought to be enough cover from those trees where they won't see you. Then fort up in those trees and wait for me."

"What are you going to do?"

"Fire and fall back. Lure them on. Now y'all hit it."

They tore off in a gallop, going down a little slope, then hitting the top of a rise and charging on for the trees. I cantered on a few more feet, then pulled out my rifle and dismounted.

The *Federales* had seen Sam and Chulo racing off and they'd come on at a gallop. I got down on one knee, holding the reins in my teeth, and carefully sighted along the barrel of my rifle at the oncoming troops. When they were about five hundred yards away, I fired. Nothing happened, they just kept coming. I adjusted my aim a little higher to allow for the slope they were coming down and fired again. A horse and rider suddenly went down. I couldn't tell if I'd hit man or animal.

That sort of slowed them down, but now they were close enough for me to sight on a man himself and not just rider and horse. I fired twice more and the second time I saw the man flip out of the saddle.

But they were getting too close and they were firing back. However, shooting from running horses is not the most accurate shooting a man is going to get off. I fired once more, heard a few bullets sing over my head in return, and then mounted up and set off at a good gallop for the creek.

I rode low over the neck of my horse. I could see the dust from the buggy wheels heading for the adobe walls, but the lay of the land hid the buggy itself.

I rode through the little creek, seeing Sam and Chulo already laying behind the low banks, pulled my horse up just outside the far line of trees, jerked my rifle out as I dismounted, and ran back up and laid beside them. The *Federales* were coming fast. They were maybe three hundred yards away. There must have been fifteen of them at first, for now I could only count thirteen.

I said to my partners, "Just hold it. All we want to do is get off a few shots, try and knock down as many of them as we can. Then we're going to break for those walls, which was about another half mile on, and fort up there. We can't make a stand here because there's not enough protection for the horses."

We watched them over the sights of our rifles. I let them come on to 200 yards, then to 100 yards. When they were just a little closer I said, "Now!"

At the first volley I saw two go down, one's horse going down with him. We got off another volley before they could even slow and one went down and then another's horse went limping off to the side and fell down. The rider must not have been hurt for he jumped in behind his horse and hid himself. They had come skidding to a halt by then and were whirling to take cover or to run. We fired two or three times more and I saw a couple more go down.

"Let's go!" I said, jumping to my feet. A few bullets were whining through the trees over our heads, but I didn't think they could hit us as disorganized as they were. We ran for the horses. I was in the lead and was almost to my mount when I heard Wilcey, right behind me, say, "Damn!"

I looked back and Wilcey was limping. Chulo came up to him, and put an arm around his back, helping him along. Wilcey was holding his right thigh. I grabbed Wilcey's horse and me and Chulo shoved him into the saddle. There was no time to see how bad Wilcey was hurt. The *Federales* were coming on faster than I'd expected and there was only time to leap into the saddle and race for the adobe ruins. Chulo and Wilcey rode in the lead, Chulo watching to see that Wilcey could ride all right. I trailed at the back and occasionally fired a pistol shot toward the *Federales*, who were already emerging from the creek bed.

We raced on. The walls were coming closer and closer. Wilcey seemed to be doing all right. He was riding low in the saddle, leaned over his horse's neck, like he should be, and he wasn't weaving or swaying. As we got within fifty yards of the walls I could see Sam leaned over one of the low walls firing cover for us. We swept in through a break in the walls, skidding our horses to a halt. I jumped down, yelling for Chulo to go help Sam at the wall. Then I ran over to Wilcey and handed him down from his horse.

"Where you hurt, buddy?" So far as I knew he'd never been shot before and that first time can kind of be a shock to your system.

He said, "Goddamn thigh." He tried to grin, but I could see he was in pain. He put an arm around my shoulder and

I helped him limp over to the safest place within the walls. I helped him down, leaning him up against the adobe, and took my pocketknife out and slit his pants up the side.

"Easy, goddamnit," he said. "I ain't over long on britches."

"I got to see," I said. I ripped his britches leg open and then breathed a little sigh of relief. The bullet had come out the front, leaving a clean hole, and it had obviously missed the bone.

"You're a lucky sonofabitch," I said. "Looks as if you might live after all."

He said, "Did you shoot me? You was the last one I heard promising to shoot me in the leg."

"If I had," I said, "I'd of missed and got you in the head. Now you lay still. I'll be right back."

I ran low over to where Chulo had tied our horses to the buggy. It was the safest part of the ruins for, in that corner, the walls were still some six feet high. But the walls of that height only ran out of the corner some ten feet either way and there was barely room for the buggy and the other horses. At the low part of the wall, to the front, Chulo and Sam were firing steadily, but not rapidly. An occasional bullet came singing overhead or thudding into the walls. I got to my horse and got the bottle of rum out of the saddlebag. Linda was huddled up against one of the buggy wheels, crying. I ran over to her, taking out my knife as I did. She looked up at me, fright suddenly showing in her face as she saw the knife. I squatted down beside her and threw up her dress. She shrunk back, fighting to keep her dress down. I pushed her hand away. "Be still, goddamnit!" I said. "I ain't got time to fuck with your silliness."

She had about three petticoats on and I picked the middle one as being the cleanest. With my knife I cut a bit swatch of it. She watched me, uncomprehending. The swatch wouldn't come loose from the hem, so I jerked it hard, almost pulling all her petticoats off, but getting the swatch I wanted. She said, "Oh, what is to become of me!"

I said, "Beats the hell out of me, lady. I'm wondering what's going to become of us." I ran back over to where Wilcey lay, carrying the rum and the big rag. He was grimacing and getting kind of white around the mouth. A gunshot wound will do that to you, especially if you ain't used to them. I uncorked the rum and told him to take a long pull. He turned it up and had a good drink. "Aaah," he said, bringing it back down. His face got a little color back.

"Hope you saved me enough for your leg," I said.

I ripped his pants back and rolled him over so I could see the hole in the back of his thigh where the bullet had gone in. I said, "This might sting a little." I had to get the rum in as deep as I could so I just up and shoved the mouth of the bottle in, pushing it until I had the neck about an inch deep. He stiffened and caught his breath. "Gaaaaaw damn!" he said. "Shiiiit!"

I let a little of the rum gurgle in and then tore off a strip of the petticoat and shoved it into the wound. I had to keep it draining so it would heal from the inside out. If you didn't do that, the outside would heal over and you'd have a festering infection inside. I knew for, until I learned, I'd had several of them myself and they ain't but one cure for it and that's a deep cut with a red-hot knife blade and you want to be as drunk as you can get when they do that. I believe I once heard a sawbones called them drainage rags tents. Never did understand why they called them that.

Wilcey was panting. I turned him back over. "Better get ready, partner, I'm coming in again."

He groaned and I shoved the neck of that bottle in the top wound and let the rum flow. I pulled it out and shoved a strip in the top one, poking it deep with my finger. He flinched, but he was already hurting so bad that a little more wasn't going to bother him. Then I took the balance of the cloth and folded it and made a bandage that I put all the way around his leg, tying it, but not too tight.

He looked up at me, trying to grin. "Looks kind of bad, don't it?"

"I've seen it look better," I said.

He said, "You got any ideas as to just what the hell we're going to do?"

NINE

I just shook my head. "Not yet, Wilcey. Let me take a look and see what the situation is. When you can, you crawl over to that back wall and keep a watch out there."

I picked up my rifle where I'd dropped it and ran bent over to where Chulo and Sam were positioned. I got in between them and peered over the top of the crumbling adobe. "What are they doing?"

"They are waiting," Chulo said.

I could see them laying in a skirmish line about 100 or 150 yards away. They had their horses back further, maybe another 200 yards, to keep them out of rifle shot.

I couldn't see them clearly, just a gray uniform every now and then against the brown grass. They were spaced out behind a little ripple in the ground, with about ten yards between each man. "How many you count?"

"There are seven," Sam said. Which seemed about right, considering the number we'd hit.

But Chulo said, quietly, "Yes, but very soon after they arrive they have a talk and then one of the *soldados* ride away."

"Oh, shit!" I said. That was trouble and bad trouble. It meant they were sending for help. No wonder they were just laying out there. They had time and time aplenty. I looked up at the sun. It was still midafternoon, still plenty of time for them to get reinforcements before dark. I said, "Have they sent anyone to the back or to the flank?"

Sam shook his head. "Not yet."

But then they didn't have to. All they had to do was trail us, out of rifle shot, wait for help to come from one way or the other, and they had us. We could run, but we couldn't hide. It didn't even matter if they thought we'd be slowed down by the buggy, and it didn't matter if they knew about Wilcey. All they had to do was bird dog us until we got to the coast and then we'd be hemmed up. No, wasn't but one thing to do and that was to get rid of them sonofabitches out in front of us. We had to kill them or scatter them so badly that we could make a clean getaway with no traces.

But I didn't quite know how to do it without a frontal charge and that would damn near be suicide, us charging against riflemen in fixed positions. They'd be sure to get some of us. And then I had a wounded man to think of. I looked back. Wilcey had gotten himself over to the rear wall, which was mostly just a rubble of adobe blocks. He had his rifle and didn't appear to be in too bad of shape.

I said, "I got to think."

As indeed I did.

I ran crouching across the space and slid down beside Wilcey. He gave me a look, half grin, half grimace. "What the hell did you do with that rum?" he asked me. "I could use a long pull."

I sprinted back over to where I'd been doctoring him, got

the rum, and got back and handed it to him. He took a long pull and some of the pain went out of his face as it hit his belly. "Goddamn, Young," he said, "when you got me into this outlaw business you didn't tell me a man could get shot."

"Listen," I said, "how are you feeling? We got to do something and fast."

"What's happened now?"

"That bunch is just laying out there. They ain't doing nothing. Chulo seen one of them ride off. It's got to be a damn good bet that they've sent for reinforcements. So we got to do something and do it damn fast. Can you ride?"

"Hell, yes," he said. "Hell, I got to be able to ride, don't I?"

I looked down at the bandage. It was getting pretty stained with blood, but the wound wasn't bleeding all that much, not enough, anyway, to make him too weak.

"We going to run for it?"

I shook my head and told him why. "They'd just bird dog us until we went to ground. We got to go kill or scatter them seven that's out there."

"How?"

"I don't know yet," I said. I took the bottle of rum out of his hand and had a pull. Then I got out a cigarillo and lit it. As I threw the match away I happened to glance toward the front of the ruins. Linda had left the buggy and was slipping, bent over, along behind Chulo and Sam, heading for what remained of the front door. I yelled, "Chulo! Behind you!"

He whirled, saw the girl, and made a dive for her. She began to run for the gate and Sam stood up, chasing her. Chulo was just ahead of him, scrambling to his feet. He made a dive for her just as she got to the doorway, bringing her down in a heap. She was screaming and beating at him with her fists, but behind them I saw Sam suddenly clutch at his shoulder and go down. "Oh, shit!" I said. I threw away my cigarillo and raced to him. He had his hand over his shoulder, and when I pulled it away, there was blood on his shoulder. I ripped the cloth open where the bullet had made a hole. My heart was in my mouth. We couldn't stand any more wounded. It was a ragged little wound, but nothing more than that. It had just cut a little furrow through the flesh of his shoulder. We'd been lucky as hell twice. I didn't know how much longer it could last. I said, disgustedly, "Go and pour some rum on that and don't be a damn fool enough to stand up anymore."

Then I made my way over to where the girl was still struggling with Chulo. I told him to get back to his post. I was angry as hell. I took her by the hair and jerked her head around and slapped her hard in the face. She stopped hollering and her eyes got big. "Listen, you bitch," I said, "you try something like that again and I'll shoot you down. You understand? You almost got one of my men killed and I'm tired of fucking with you." I drew back my hand to slap her again. "Now get your ass back there to that buggy before I do shoot you."

I let go her hair and she got to her feet and ran over and slumped down against the buggy, looking back at me fearfully. They hadn't fired a shot, even though when she'd run back, she'd been in full view of those troops.

I went back and sat by Wilcey and lit a cigarillo to replace the one I hadn't smoked.

He said, "Why the hell didn't you let her go, Will? Goddamn, Sam nearly got kilt!"

I said, "Because she's the only hostage we got left and she's going to be our ticket out of here."

I was thinking about how she'd run by that low wall and they hadn't fired.

He said, "Hell, they ain't going to negotiate and you ain't

got Don Bustamante here to make them. What the hell good is she to us?"

"Let me think it all out," I said. "Hand me that rum."

Sam had gone back to the wall. He called to me. "Hey, Wilson, we're getting low on water."

"And that ain't all," Wilcey said. "About out of luck."

I didn't say anything, just sat there thinking and sipping at the rum. It seemed like it was falling into place. I said to Wilcey, "I got an idea."

"What?"

I told him about it. He looked kind of doubtful. "Sounds kind of risky to me. You know them goddamn *Meskin* soldiers is goddamn excitable. Besides, you sure you can do that?" He had the bottle of rum in his hand, and he jabbed it toward where Linda was slumped down on the ground by the buggy. "I mean, I damn near fainted when you slapped her."

"Leave that part out of it. If we don't do this, I ain't got no other ideas. You got any?"

He shook his head.

"Then we got to try it."

Ignoring Linda, I got up and went over and studied the buggy. It was just one of them common one-horse buggies that well-off people drive. It had a canopy over the top to keep out the rain and sun; it was made, I supposed, out of some kind of canvas with tar on it to make it waterproof, and then shined up with black paint. The canopy had a little round window in the back with isin-glass so the driver could see where he'd been. And there was a little wooden bench in the back, right behind the canopy where they could carry an extra passenger or a servant. There was also a bunch of straps running up the back to the roof for securing parcels and luggage and such. I'd noticed some broken planks laying around, and I got a couple of them and they tied on pretty nicely with the straps. I got a few more and just ran them right on up the back. It made a pretty solid shield with those planks there. Of course they didn't give no protection for whoever was in the front.

Then I went and got my lariat rope and uncoiled it and taken out my clasp knife and cut a hole through the canopy canvas between two of the planks and run the loop end of my lariat through the hole. Out of the corner of my eye I could see Chulo and Sam watching me. I imagine they were wondering what the hell I was up to. Below me, Linda was staring up, probably wondering the same thing. I got her by the arm and lifted her into the seat, then made a loop and put it over her head and around her waist.

"Don't move," I said to her. "Don't dare move."

I crawled over to where Sam and Chulo were. Then I yelled at Wilcey and motioned for him to come over. He came slowly, his leg painful, just kind of scuttling along.

"Que pasa?" Chulo asked me.

I said, "We're getting out of here. I hope."

Sam said, "How?"

I told them. I finished by saying, "Hell, it's a chance. And right now our chances don't look so good. We can't run and we can't just up and charge them. We could wait until night and try and slip away, but my guess is that help will be here long before then." I looked up at the sun. "It's still a good three, four hours till dusk, and I think the reinforcements will be here within the next hour or hour and a half. We could stay here and try and hold out, but we're low on water, out of food, and pretty soon we'd be out of cartridges. We could use the woman as a hostage as we did back in Sabinas Hidalgo, but that won't work with just one hostage. When you got a bunch, you can kill one to show them you ain't bluffing. But when you just got one and they call your bluff, what do you do then?" I shrugged. "So them is our chances. What do y'all think?"

Sam said, "Hell, I think it's a damn good idear."

Chulo grinned, his teeth big in his black face. *"Como, no?* Chulo is growing tired of these little men with rifles shooting at him."

Wilcey said, "Hell, Will, I'm like you. I ain't got no better ideas, and this appears to give us pretty good chance. I just—" he stopped.

"What?"

"Oh, nothing. You know she might get hurt."

I said, "All right. Let's get to it. Remember, we got to get that buggy lined up in front of that gate with all of us a-horseback behind it before we go out the opening. Sam, you turn it around and then get mounted on your own horse. Ever'body check their weapons for full loads."

When Sam had the buggy turned, I walked up to Linda and handed her the reins. "Now, woman," I said, "you are going to drive this buggy straight at them troops on the prairie. You got that?"

She just looked bewildered.

I said, "You're going to keep that horse in a trot. We're all going to be right behind you and . . ." I touched the rope around her waist, "I'll have hold of the other end of this. If you don't drive just as straight at them as you can, or if you try and jump off and run, I'll snatch back so hard on that thing that you'll never breathe again. You *sabe*?"

Fright was starting to replace the bewilderment in her eyes. She said, "Toward the *Federales?* I am to drive the buggy? And you will be behind?"

"That's right, lady."

"But perhaps they will shoot!"

I said, grimly, "You better hope they don't. And for your sake and for ours I hope they don't either. Now take these reins and start driving when I give the word. If you want to get out of this alive, you better do exactly as I told you."

She took the reins, her face gone white under the dust.

The others were mounted and now I swung up on my mount and reached down and got the coil of my lariat rope. I give it a tug to let her know I was there. We'd position the buggy in the back corner of the walls so that we could make a quick left and be lined up almost dead on the gate. Sam and I were in the first line with Chulo and Wilcey riding tandem right behind us.

I looked at them. "Ready?"

They nodded and I flicked the lariat. "Start driving, Senora Bustamante. And remember, right straight at them."

There was a second before we were lined out that we were exposed, but not a shot was fired. Then we were out the opening and rolling toward the skirmish line of soldiers. We were riding low on our horses, which kept our heads below the canopy of the buggy, but even riding as close together as possible, we were still a little exposed on each side.

After we had gone perhaps thirty yards, I hazarded a quick look around the side of the buggy. The *Federales* were up on one knee, their rifles up. I was expecting them to start shooting at any moment, but then I saw one of them waving his sword, an officer, I guess, waving at his men. I hoped that he'd seen it was the Senora Bustamante driving the buggy and was telling them not to fire.

We come on at a good pace. I could see how confused they were getting. When we were still a hundred yards away, they commenced to sort of fall back, looking as if they didn't quite know what the hell to do. I flicked the lariat and yelled at Linda. "Faster!"

She slapped the horse and we hit a canter. I told my partners, "Remember, shoot as many of the soldiers as you can, but when they begin scattering, start shooting at their horses. The more of them you kill the less that's going to be on our trail."

I raised up in my stirrups to look over the top of the canopy. They were really falling back now. It was time to start shooting. "Fire!" I said. Sam and I were shooting over the top of the canopy, and Wilcey and Chulo were firing around the sides. I fired rapidly with my rifle, concentrating on the first man I got in my sights. He went down and I got another with a single shot. They were running. As we got closer, first one and then the other turned his back and began to run, heading for their horses. I saw another fall, and then another. There were only three of them fleeing now, and we were rapidly closing the gap. One turned, dropped to one knee, and leveled his rifle, but before he could get off a shot, somebody got him solid in the chest and he flipped over on his back. I yelled, "Fire at the horses!"

My rifle was empty so I jerked out my revolver and began firing rapidly at the *Federales'* horses. One went down, but the others began breaking their picket lines and running in all directions.

I yelled, "Let's vamoose!"

We wheeled around leaving the buggy clattering on. I just simply dropped the rope. The *Federales* had not fired a single shot at us.

I put us in a hard gallop, taking a northwesterly direction to throw off anyone who might be watching which way we were heading. As soon as we dropped the remaining soldiers down behind the horizon, I intended to turn us on a southern heading. As we raced over the prairie, flying by our late fort, the adobe walls, I took a look back over my shoulder. The last I saw of Linda she had that buggy horse in a good gallop, going away from me. I laughed. By the time they got themselves organized we'd have a big head start.

TEN

Two nights later we were camped on a little hill over-looking Tampico with the lights of the city before us. We'd found a little town on the coast a few miles down and had sent Chulo in to bring us back a supply of rum and grub. Now we were sitting around the campfire we'd built, eating beef and beans and tortillas and drinking rum and water. We were feeling pretty good. Wilcey's gunshot wound had done fine. It didn't show any signs of getting infected. First night it had been a little red so I'd pulled out the tents, taken a red-hot knife and kind of cauterized the mouth, and then poured in rum. Wilcey had carried on pretty good, but I had Chulo and Sam to hold him down.

We'd had some pretty good laughs about the way the *Federales* had acted when we'd, as Wilcey put it, "attacked them with a buggy." Chulo had said, "They run and they run, but they don't shoot!"

Bustamante the junior had had the last laugh. He'd

shorted us on the money. Instead of bringing us $20,000, he'd only brought $19,600.

Sam said, "Maybe in his excitement and fear he miscount."

Wilcey said, "Miscounted hell! The man's a thief. He done it deliberately. He didn't do nothin' but put the extra four hundred dollars in his pocket."

But, what with the $2,000 we'd taken off of Martin, it hadn't been a bad haul at that.

"Not a bad swap," Sam said, laughing. "A hamstring for two thousand dollars."

And Chulo laughed and said, "I like to hamstring one *Meskin.*"

Oh, he was a mean one all right.

We were all in a good mood and looking forward to going into Tampico and having some good times. I figured it would be all right if we wandered in one by one and didn't act like we knew each other. The authorities were looking for four men, and Tampico being a shipping port, there were plenty of hardcase-looking gringos wandering around there, so if we didn't gather up, we wouldn't draw no attention.

But I did have to tell Wilcey he couldn't go to no whorehouse. "You can't be taking your britches down and letting some girl see that bloody bandage. There'd be talk. You just content yourself with drinking and playing cards."

He hadn't liked it, but he'd seen the sense of it.

Later that night, when he and I were off a little ways from the others, he said, "You know, I still can't believe you did what you did with that girl."

"What do you mean?"

We were leaned back comfortably, smoking. There was a cool breeze blowing in off the sea and enough moonlight so you didn't feel like you were inside a cow.

"Well, here's this woman you'd pined for for I don't

know how many years. Hell, you was even going to shoot
me if I'd taken one more step toward her. And the next thing
you're slapping her around and tying her in the front seat of
a buggy to face a bunch of trigger-happy *Meskins*. I don't
know, somehow it just didn't seem your style."

I laughed. "Say, what is my style, anyway?"

He thought. "Oh, I don't know. You're plenty mean, but
you ain't mean like Chulo is. I guess I'd have to say you got
a sense of honor."

"Well, I didn't fuck her when I could have. That was
pretty honorable."

"Yes, I guess it was."

We were silent a moment and then he said, "What would
you have done if them *Meskins* had started shooting at the
buggy?"

I said, "I pretty well figured they wouldn't. I seen how
they didn't shoot when she run by that low wall, so I figured
they had strict orders not to endanger her."

He insisted. "But what if they had?"

"What difference does it make now?"

"What would you have done?"

I said, "I'd have cut straight left and drawn their fire."

He was silent a moment and then he said, "That's what
me and Chulo was both afraid you'd do."

We went into Tampico next day and had a good time
without getting into trouble. There was an American steamship laying at anchor that was bound for Galveston, Texas,
in two days. We all booked passage on her. All, that is,
except Sam Owl, who felt that Texas might still be a little
warm for him.

Well, it was still pretty warm for me, too, but so was
Mexico, and I didn't feel like they'd be looking for me in
such a place as Galveston. Besides, I wanted to get a look at
Houston, which I'd heard was getting to be quite the city. I

figured with all the people they said lived there a man would be hard to spot. But, then, the more people the more law. So I guess it was still acey-deucey.

We spent the two days whoring and drinking and gambling and then boarded the steamship without incident.

As the steamer got out into the bay, Wilcey and I stood at the stern railing, watching the city of Tampico growing smaller and smaller.

Wilcey said, "You still going to miss her, Will?"

I shook my head. "No."

"Why not?"

I shrugged. "Because there was never anything there. How can you miss something that never was."

I watched the blue water being chopped to a froth by the giant paddle wheels of the steamer, thinking of going into the ship's saloon and having a drink.

I said, "Let's go in and have a morning whiskey."

He said, "Sounds like a damn good idea. I believe we owe it to ourselves."

We went on into the saloon, which was open even at that hour of the morning. What the hell, I had everything right to be feeling good. I was free and my pockets was full of somebody else's money and that's about all an outlaw can want or expect.